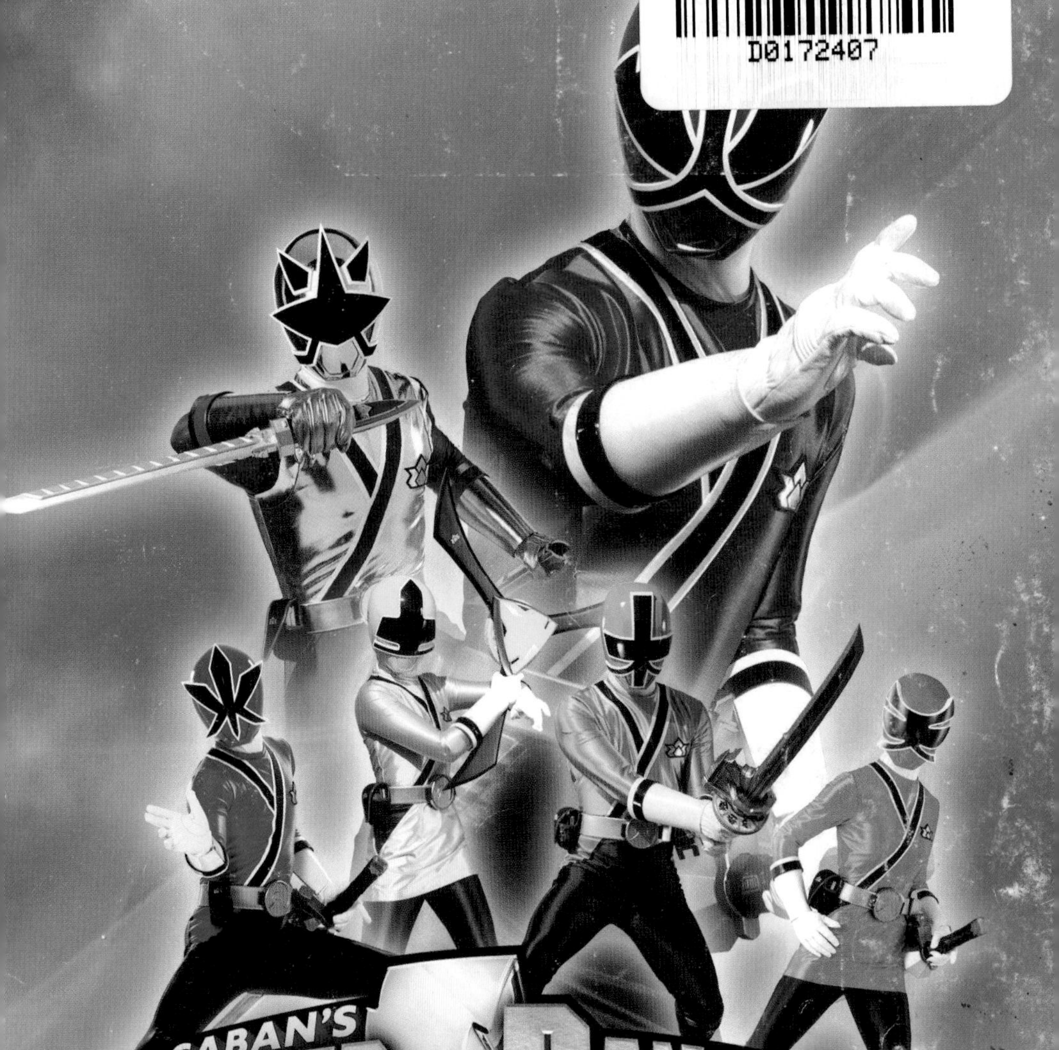

SABAN'S POWER RANGERS SUPER SAMURAI™

PAPERCUTZ™

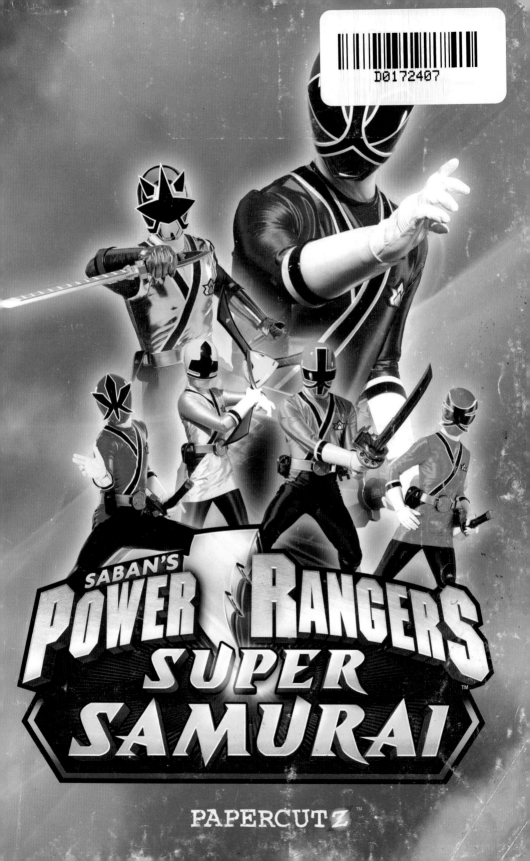

SABAN'S POWER RANGERS SUPER SAMURAI

Graphic Novels Available From PAPERCUTZ

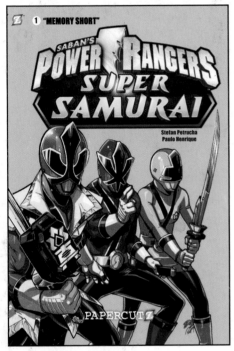

1 "MEMORY SHORT"
SABAN'S POWER RANGERS SUPER SAMURAI
Stefan Petrucha
Paulo Henrique
PAPERCUTZ

Graphic Novel #1

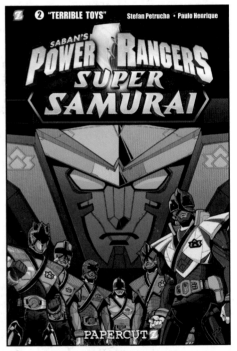

2 "TERRIBLE TOYS"
Stefan Petrucha • Paulo Henrique
SABAN'S POWER RANGERS SUPER SAMURAI
PAPERCUTZ

Graphic Novel #2

POWER RANGERS graphic novels are available for $6.99 each in paperback, and $10.99 in hardcover. Available from booksellers everywhere. You can also order online from www.papercutz.com. Or call 1-800-886-1223, Monday through Fridays, 9 – 5 EST. MC, Visa, and AmEx accepted. To order by mail, please add $4.00 for postage and handling for first book ordered, $1.00 for each additional book and make check payable to NBM Publishing. Send to: Papercutz, 160 Broadway, Suite 700, East Wing, New York, NY 100038.

② "TERRIBLE TOYS"

Stefan Petrucha – Writer
Paulo Henrique – Artist
Laurie E. Smith – Colorist

PAPERCUTZ™
New York

SABAN'S POWER RANGERS SUPER SAMURAI
#2 "TERRIBLE TOYS"

STEFAN PETRUCHA – Writer
PAULO HENRIQUE – Artist
LAURIE E. SMITH – Colorist
BRYAN SENKA – Letterer

Production by NELSON DESIGN GROUP, LLC
Associate Editor – MICHAEL PETRANEK
JIM SALICRUP
Editor-in-Chief

ISBN: 978-1-59707-338-7 paperback edition
ISBN: 978-1-59707-339-4 hardcover edition

Printed in Canada
October 2012 by Friesens Printing
1 Printers Way
Altona, MB R0G 0B0

Distributed by Macmillan

First Printing

MEET

SABAN'S POWER RANGERS SUPER SAMURAI

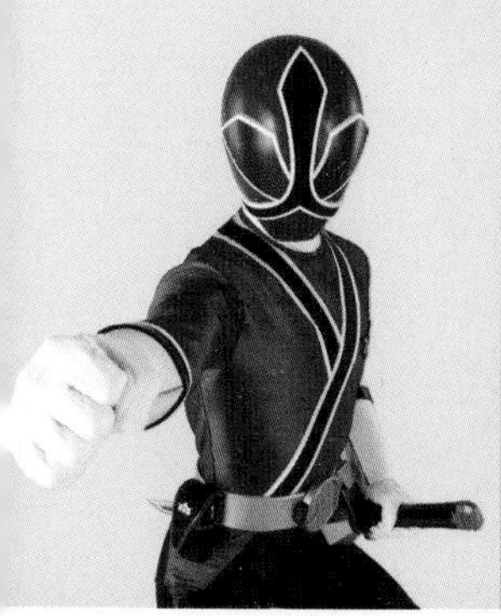

For as long as the Nighlok have existed, there have been Power Rangers sworn to fight them.

The current team of Samurai Power Rangers is a group of teens who grew up knowing that one day they would be summoned to use their uniquely inherited powers and extraordinary skills against evil as the Power Rangers. These skills and powers have been passed down through generation to generation and determine which Ranger they will become.

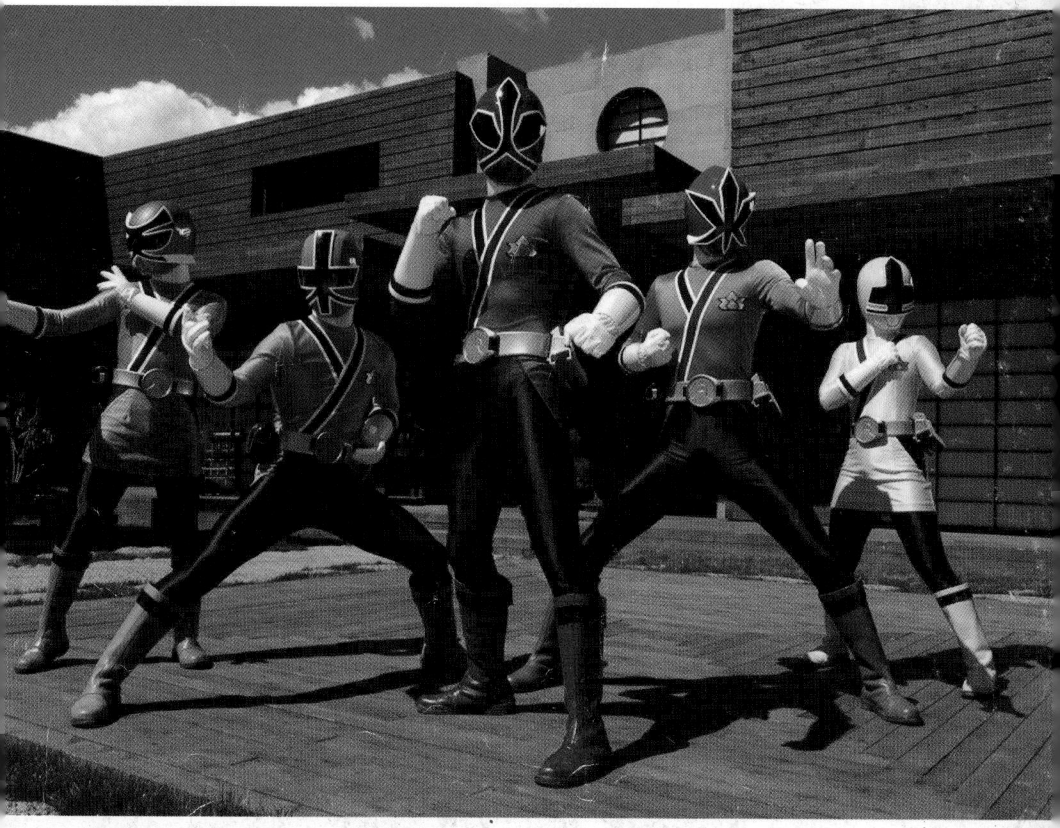

THE RED RANGER (JAYDEN)

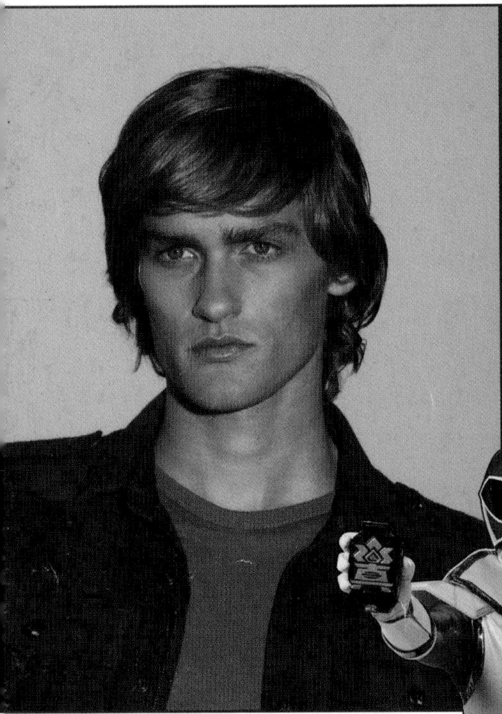

Jayden, the Red Ranger, is the leader of the Samurai Power Rangers. He is a man of few words, but when he speaks he means what he says. He was raised by Mentor Ji after his father died, who was the Red Ranger before him. Jayden has become an excellent warrior and has kept the Moogers at bay on his own for some time. Now, with the help of the other Rangers, Jayden is learning to be a leader and what it is like to have true friends.

Jayden is a kind and caring person but can be firm when action calls. He also carries a secret that he cannot reveal to the other Rangers and at times this knowledge causes him conflict.

His element is fire and his Zord is the Lion.

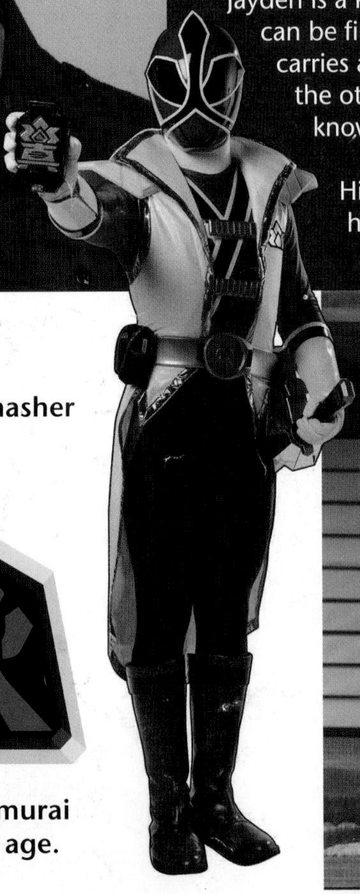

Weapon:
Spin Sword/Fire Smasher

Signature Move:
Fire Smasher!

Element:
Fire

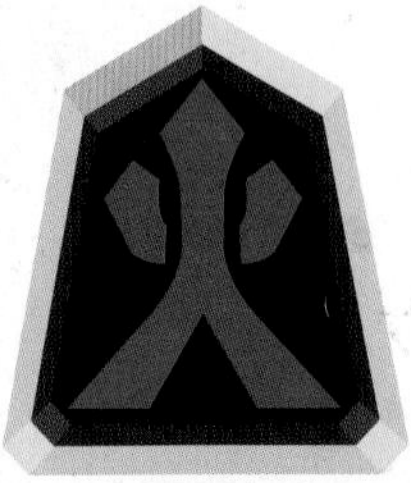

Zord:
Lion

Notes:
Trained to be a Samurai from a very young age.

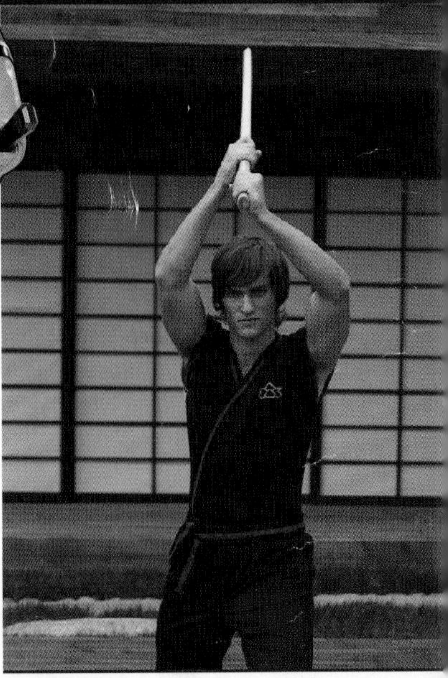

THE PINK RANGER (MIA)

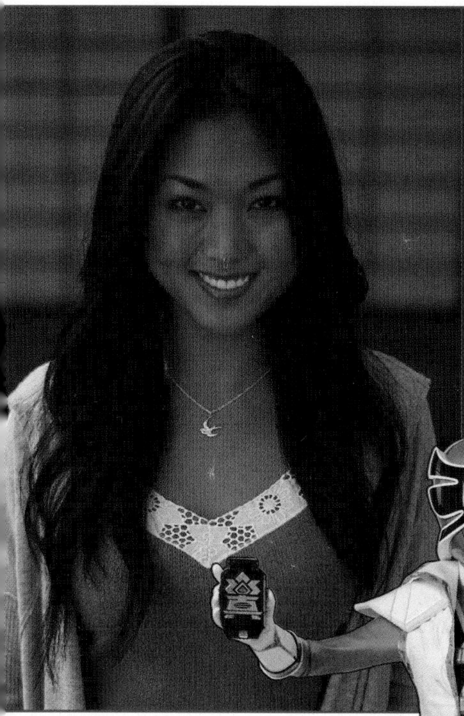

Mia, the Pink Ranger, is the big sister to the group. She is a confident, intuitive, and sensitive person. She is very pragmatic and cares a lot about the well-being of the other Rangers. She trains as hard as the rest of the team, and will jump in to help any Ranger or person in need.

Mia enjoys cooking and often offers up her skills to feed the other Rangers. Problem is that Mia is not a good cook. The humor begins as the other Rangers try their best to act as if her culinary delights are edible.

Mia's element is the sky and her Zord is the Turtle.

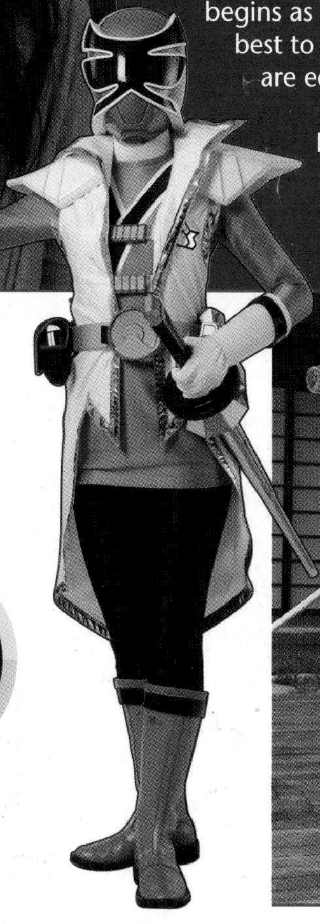

Weapon:
Spin Sword/Sky Fan

Signature Move:
Airway!

Element:
Sky

天

Zord:
Turtle

Notes:
Longs to be a gourmet chef and used to sing

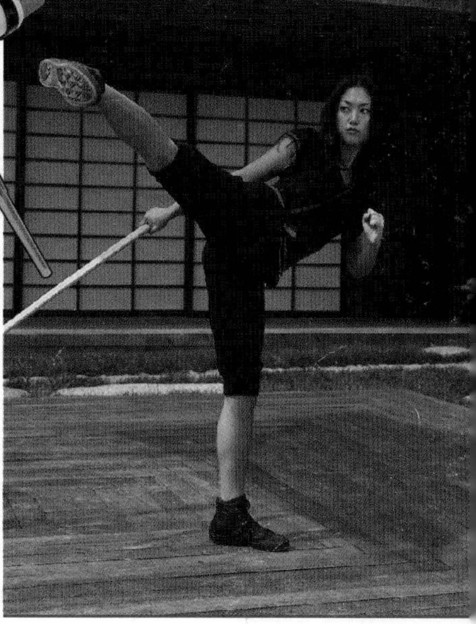

THE BLUE RANGER (KEVIN)

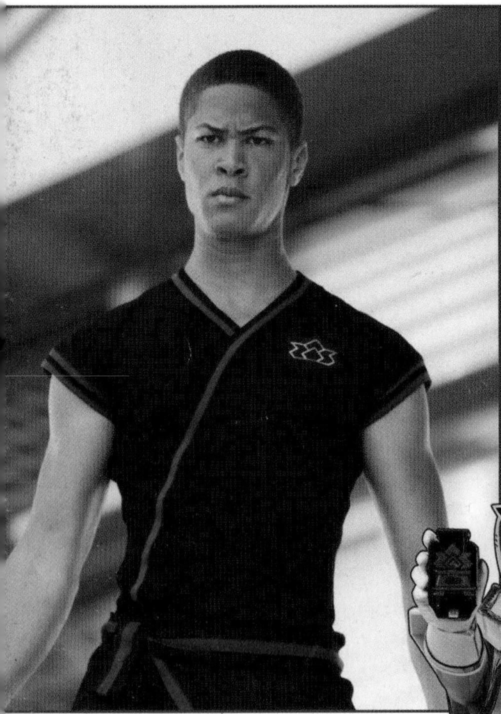

Kevin, the Blue Ranger, has lived his entire life by the code of the Samurai.

Kevin's dream was to be an Olympic swimmer. However, he has placed that dream on hold to become the Blue Ranger. He is a well-trained swordsman and has been raised on the traditions of the Samurai. Kevin is the more sober Ranger who continues his discipline with a daily workout and training. He is honored to be a Samurai and takes his position among the Rangers seriously.

His element is water and his Zord is the Dragon.

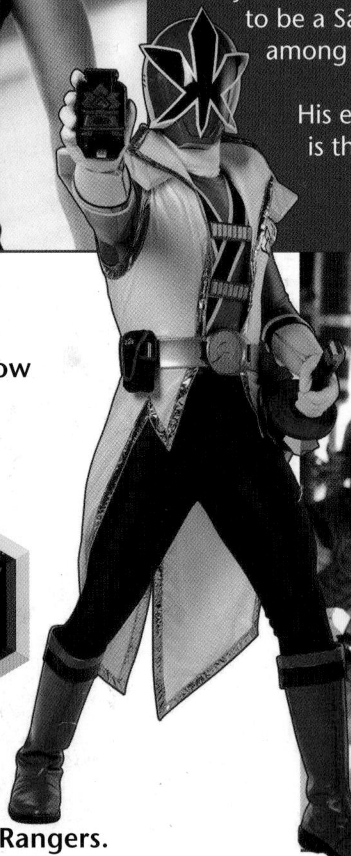

Weapon:
Spin Sword/Hydro Bow

Signature Move:
Dragon Splash!

Element:
Water

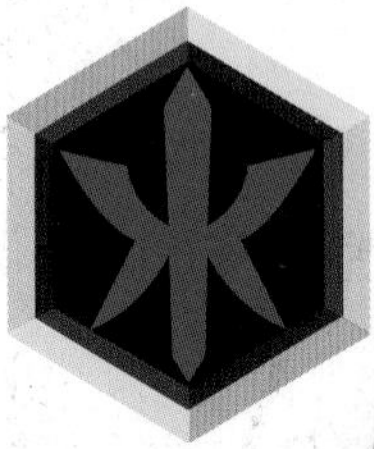

Zord:
Dragon

Notes:
Aside from Jayden, Kevin has the best technique of all the Rangers.

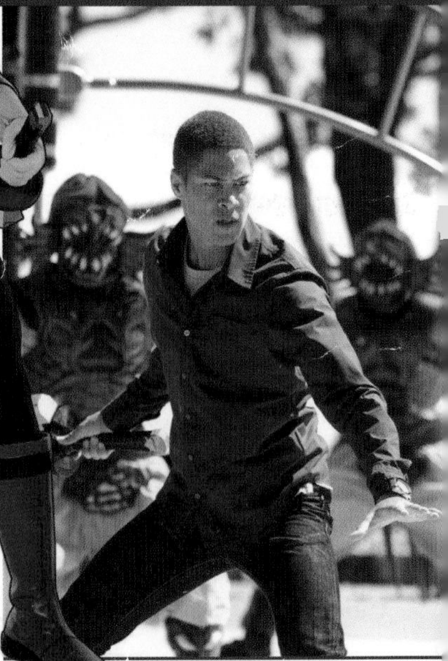

THE GREEN RANGER (MIKE)

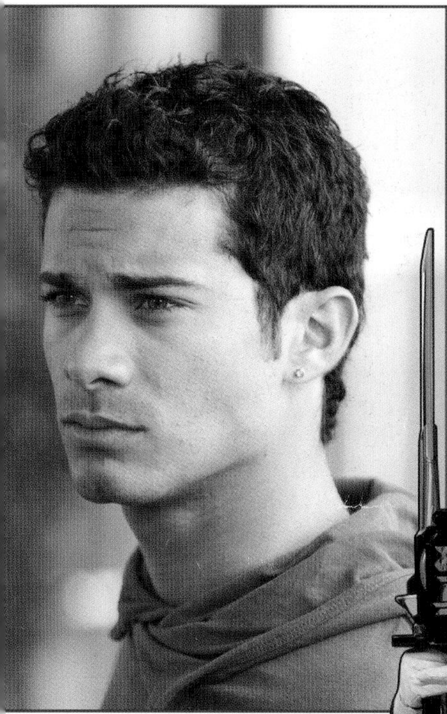

Being a bit of a rebel is truly part of Mike's nature. He is the Green Ranger.

Mike loves to think outside of the box, play video games, and hang with friends. He has a more casual approach to his training but deep down inside takes being a Power Ranger seriously. He is a free spirit and has a great sense of humor. All of his characteristics allow him to come up with new fighting strategies to beat Master Xandred's evil Nighlok. He is a valuable part of the team.

Mike's element is the forest and his Zord is the Bear.

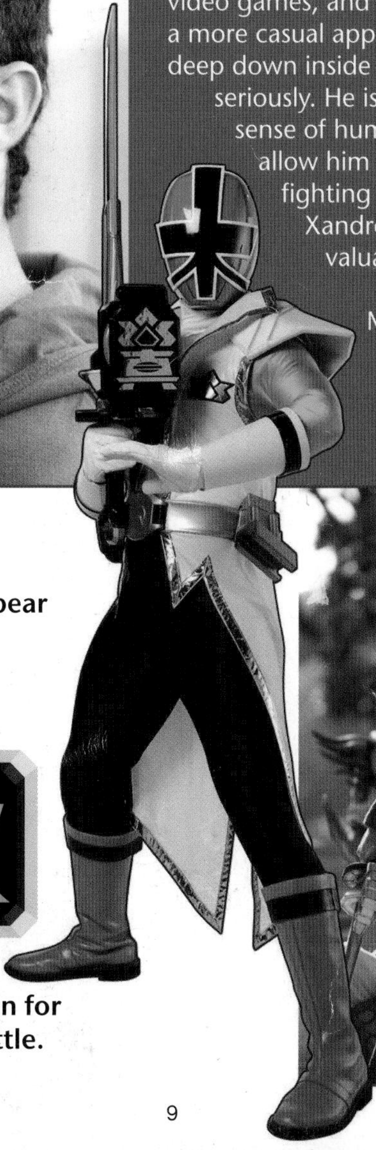

Weapon:
Spin Sword, Forest Spear

Signature Move:
Forest Vortex!

Element:
Forest

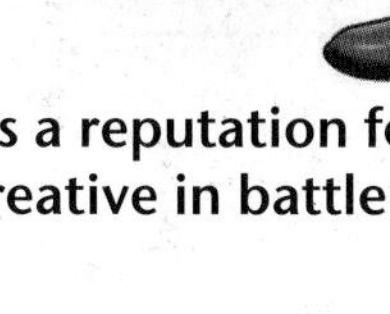

Zord:
Bear

Notes:
Mike has a reputation for being creative in battle.

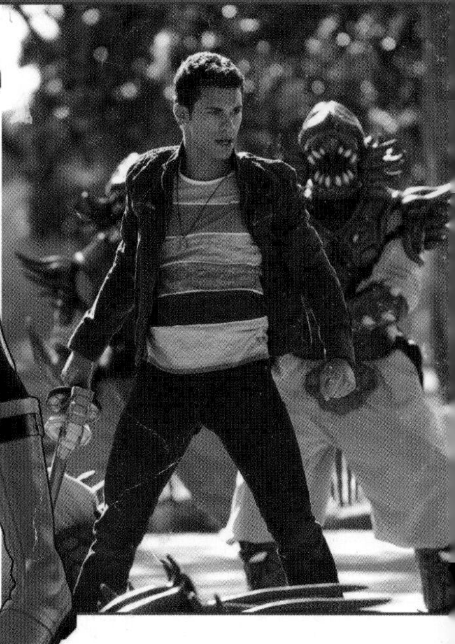

THE YELLOW RANGER (EMILY)

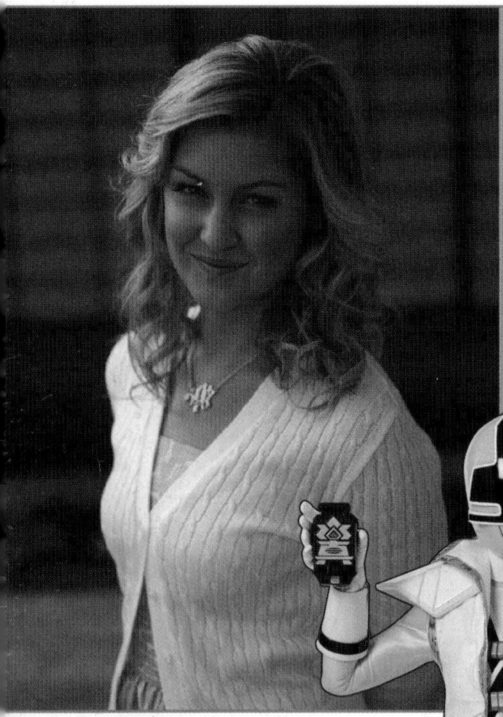

Youngest of the Rangers, Emily is the Yellow Ranger. She is a sweet and kind person who was raised in the countryside.

It was actually her sister who was originally to become the Yellow Ranger prior to falling ill. Emily stepped up to the challenge and took her sister's spot on the team. She is determined to make her sister proud and trains harder because of that. She is very musical, and her silliness is infectious. Her wide-eyed optimism often helps the team stay positive when it seems that all the odds are against them.

Emily's element is Earth and her Zord is the Ape.

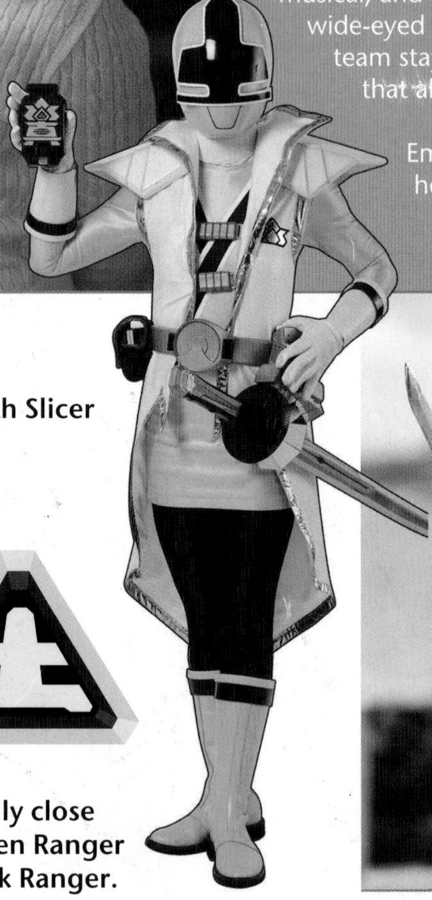

Weapon:
Spin Sword/Earth Slicer

Signature Move:
Seismic Swing!

Element:
Earth

Zord:
Ape

Notes:
Emily is especially close to Mike the Green Ranger and Mia the Pink Ranger.

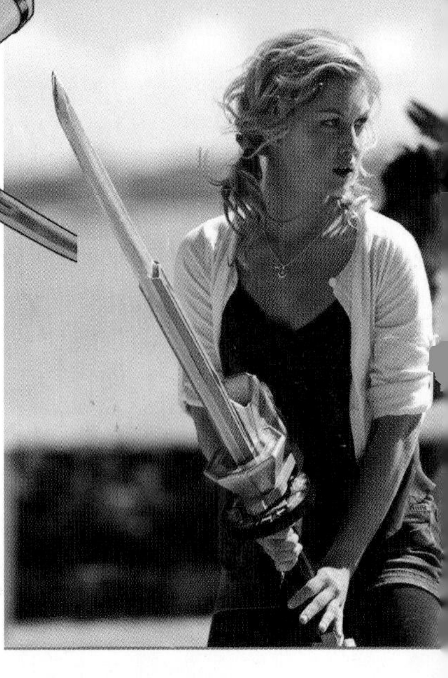

SABAN'S POWER RANGERS SUPER SAMURAI

THE GOLD RANGER (ANTONIO)

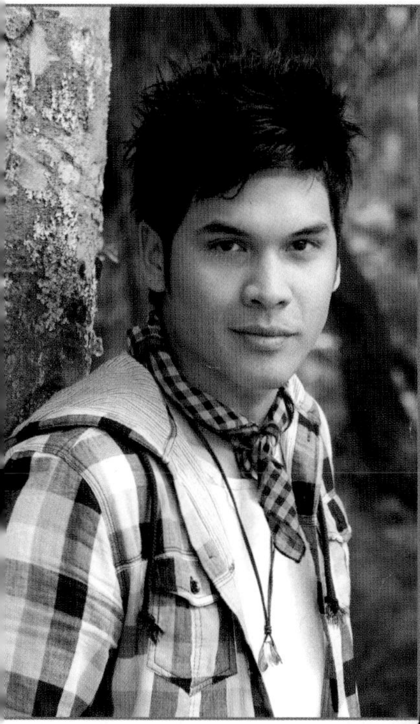

Antonio is not like the rest of the Power Rangers and is uniquely the Gold Ranger.

Unlike the other five Power Rangers, Antonio did not receive any formal Samurai training and mastered his fighting skills on his own. When he was a young child, he and Jayden were best friends. They practiced the Samurai moves together, but then Antonio's family moved away. Antonio vowed to return and to become a Samurai Power Ranger. Using his computer skills, Antonio was able to create his own Samuraizer, able to program powers and operate his OctoZord which was a present from Jayden years before. True to his word, Antonio returns as the Gold Ranger with mastered samurai skills.

His element is light and his Zord is an Octopus known as OctoZord.

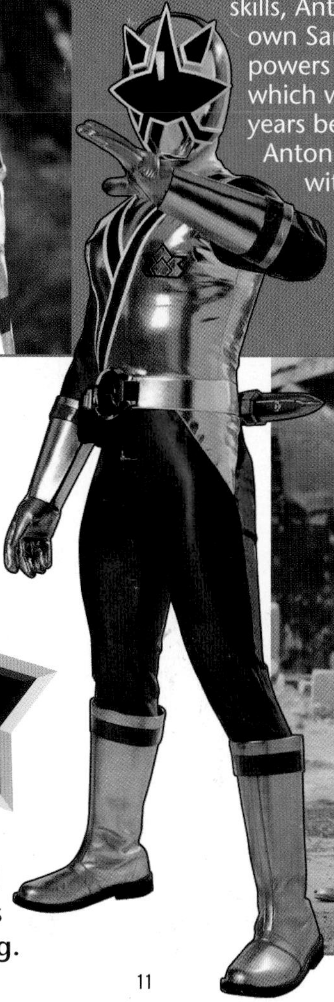

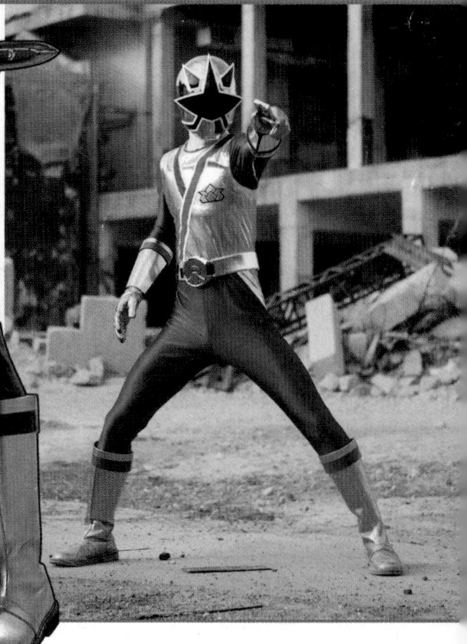

Weapon:
Barracuda Blade

Signature Move:
Barracuda Bite!

Element:
Light

Zord:
OctoZord,
LightZord

Notes:
Antonio is a techie and communicates with his Zord via text messaging.

SABAN'S POWER RANGERS SUPER SAMURAI

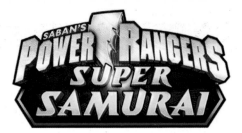

MASTER XANDRED

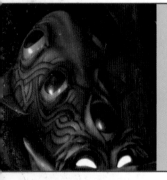

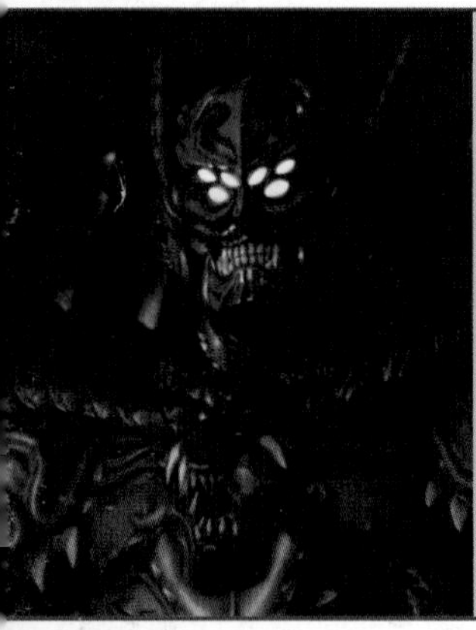

Master Xandred is the leader of the Nighlok Monsters who inhabit the Netherworld.

Jayden's Father, the previous Red Ranger, shattered Master Xandred into a million pieces, vanishing him to the Netherworld forever. Recently Master Xandred awoke and began a reign of terror in an attempt to return to our world. With his trusty advisor, Master Xandred has sent Nighlok to Earth in an attempt to make the humans cry as their tears help raise the Sanzu River. Once the river is high enough, Master Xandred can escape the Netherworld and rule the Earth.

OCTOROO

Octoroo is Master Xandred's trusted advisor. He counsels Master Xandred about the Netherworld and the Nighlok that live there. Often he offers up new plans and tactics to defeat the Rangers. Octoroo is an Octopus-like creature and at times cannot be trusted.

DAYU

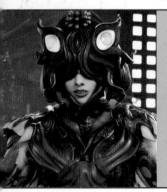

Dayu has not always been half human and half Nighlok. She once was a new bride, but she traded her human life centuries ago in an effort to save her husband as a powerful Nighlok promised to spare her husband if she would go with him. The only possession she was allowed to take with her was her guitar which became the "Harmonium." Master Xandred keeps her near because her music soothes him.

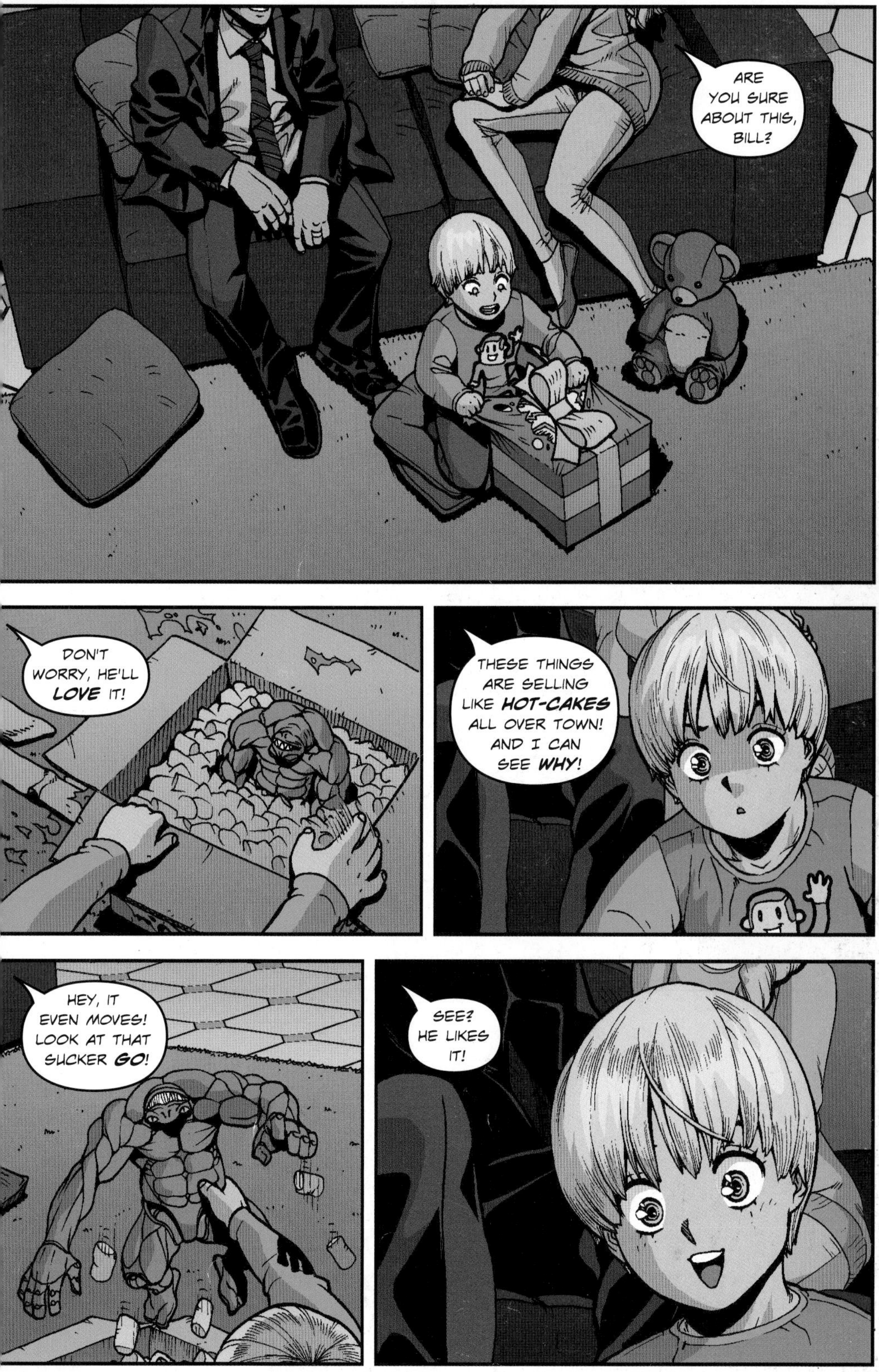
ARE YOU SURE ABOUT THIS, BILL?
DON'T WORRY, HE'LL **LOVE** IT!
THESE THINGS ARE SELLING LIKE **HOT-CAKES** ALL OVER TOWN! AND I CAN SEE **WHY**!
HEY, IT EVEN MOVES! LOOK AT THAT SUCKER **GO**!
SEE? HE LIKES IT!

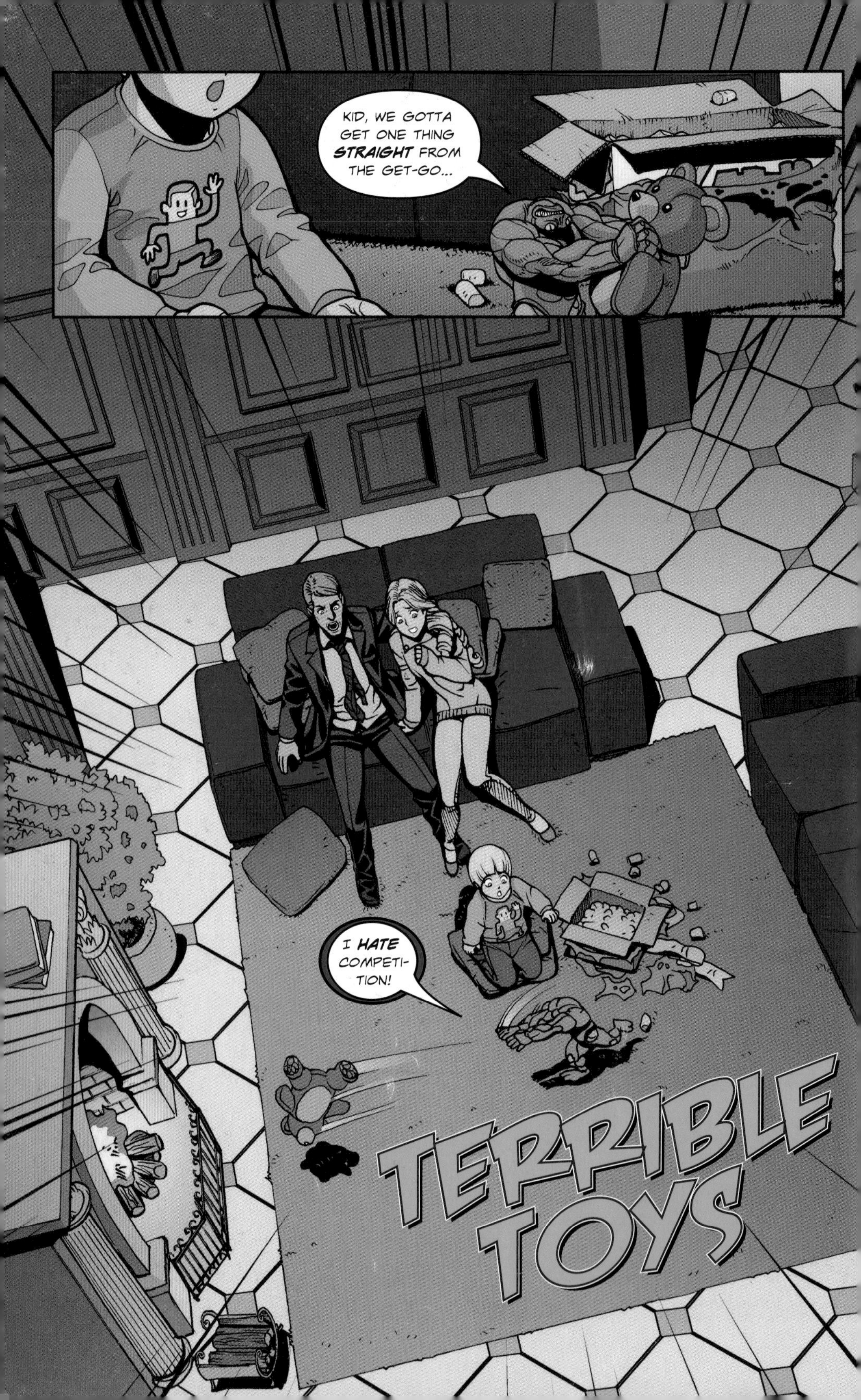
KID, WE GOTTA GET ONE THING STRAIGHT FROM THE GET-GO...
I HATE COMPETITION!
TERRIBLE TOYS

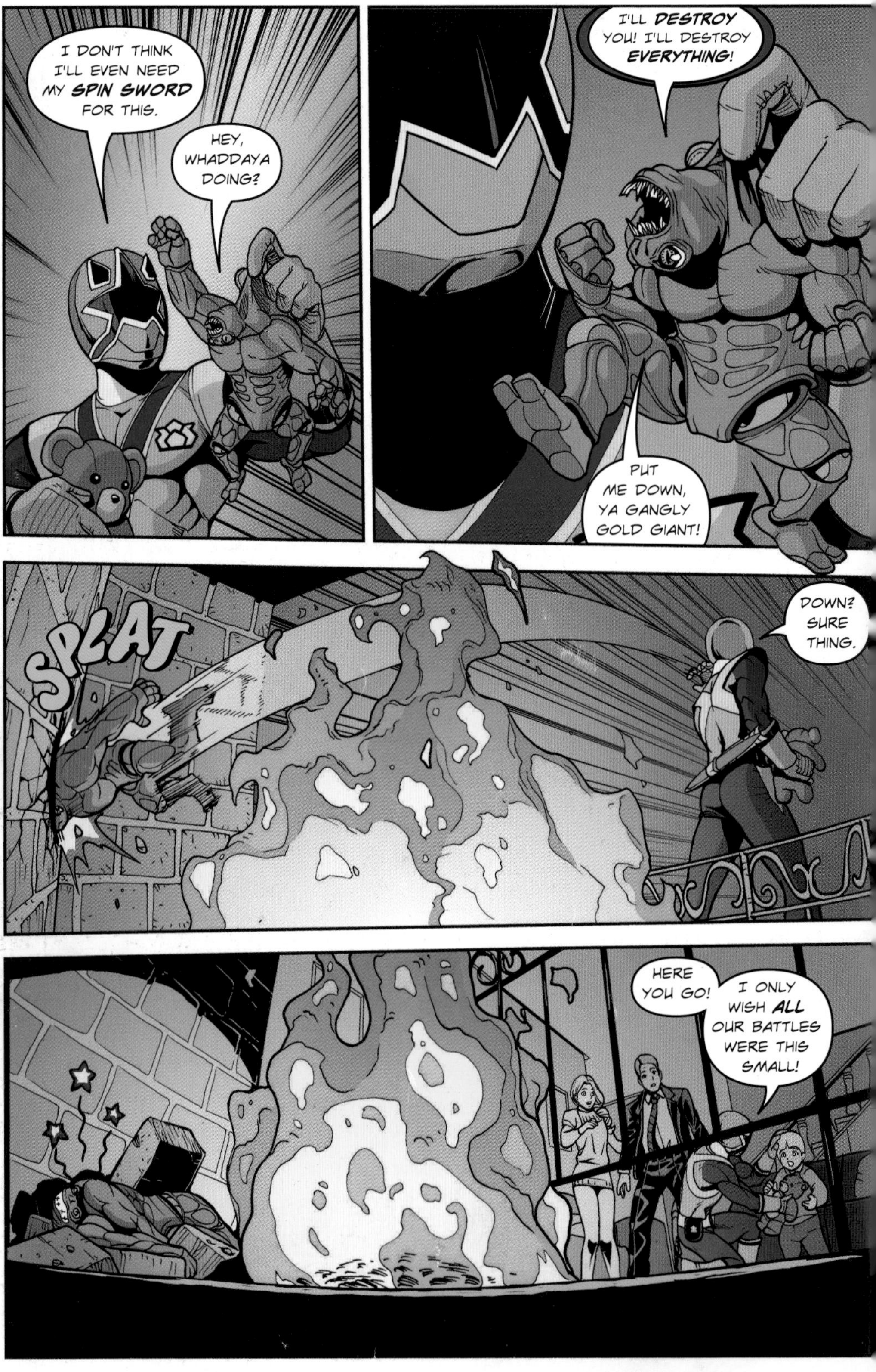
I DON'T THINK I'LL EVEN NEED MY **SPIN SWORD** FOR THIS.
HEY, WHADDAYA DOING?
I'LL **DESTROY** YOU! I'LL DESTROY **EVERYTHING**!
PUT ME DOWN, YA GANGLY GOLD GIANT!
DOWN? SURE THING.
SPLAT
HERE YOU GO!
I ONLY WISH **ALL** OUR BATTLES WERE THIS SMALL!

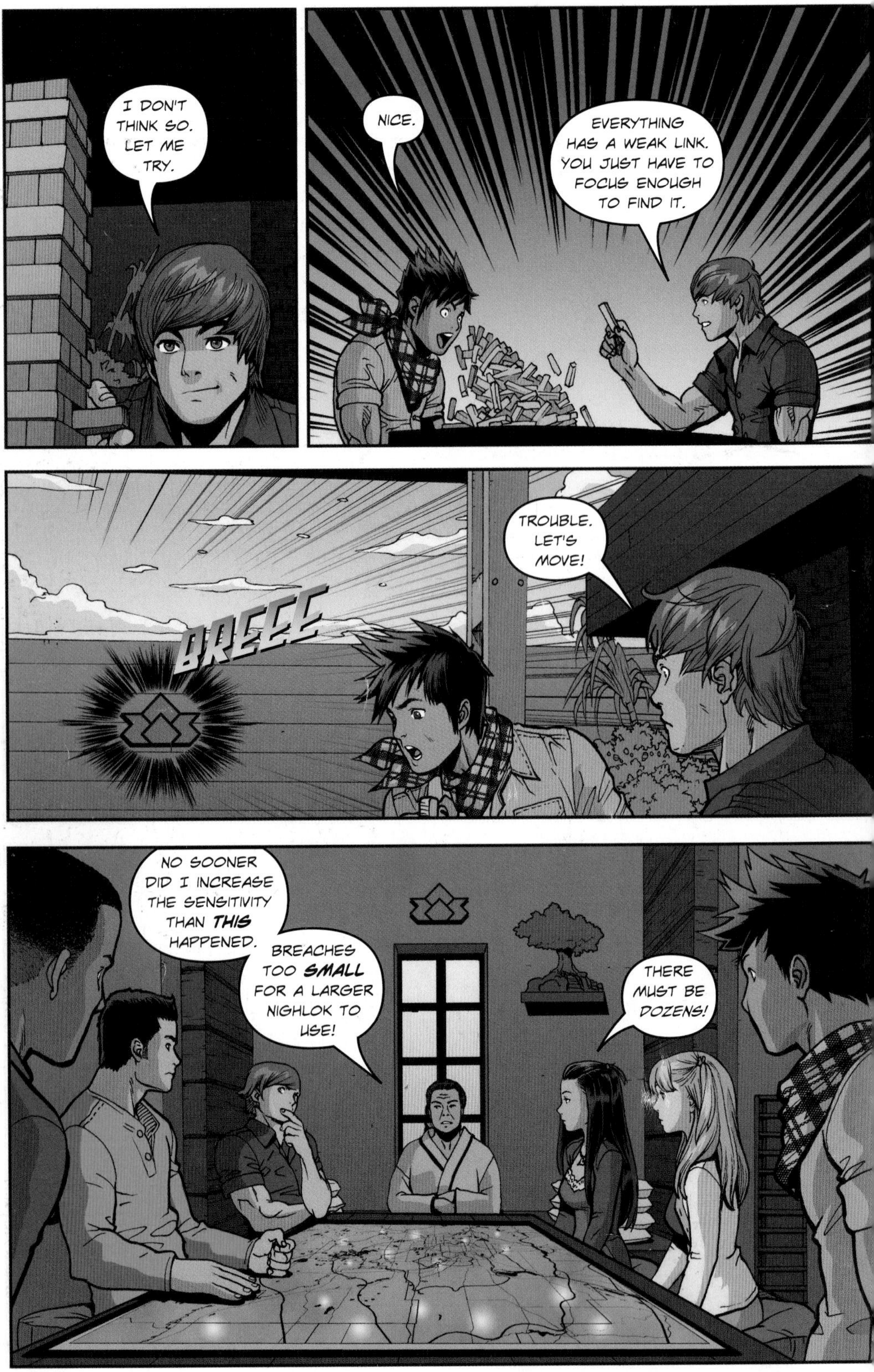
I DON'T THINK SO. LET ME TRY.
NICE.
EVERYTHING HAS A WEAK LINK. YOU JUST HAVE TO FOCUS ENOUGH TO FIND IT.
BREEE
TROUBLE. LET'S MOVE!
NO SOONER DID I INCREASE THE SENSITIVITY THAN THIS HAPPENED.
BREACHES TOO SMALL FOR A LARGER NIGHLOK TO USE!
THERE MUST BE DOZENS!

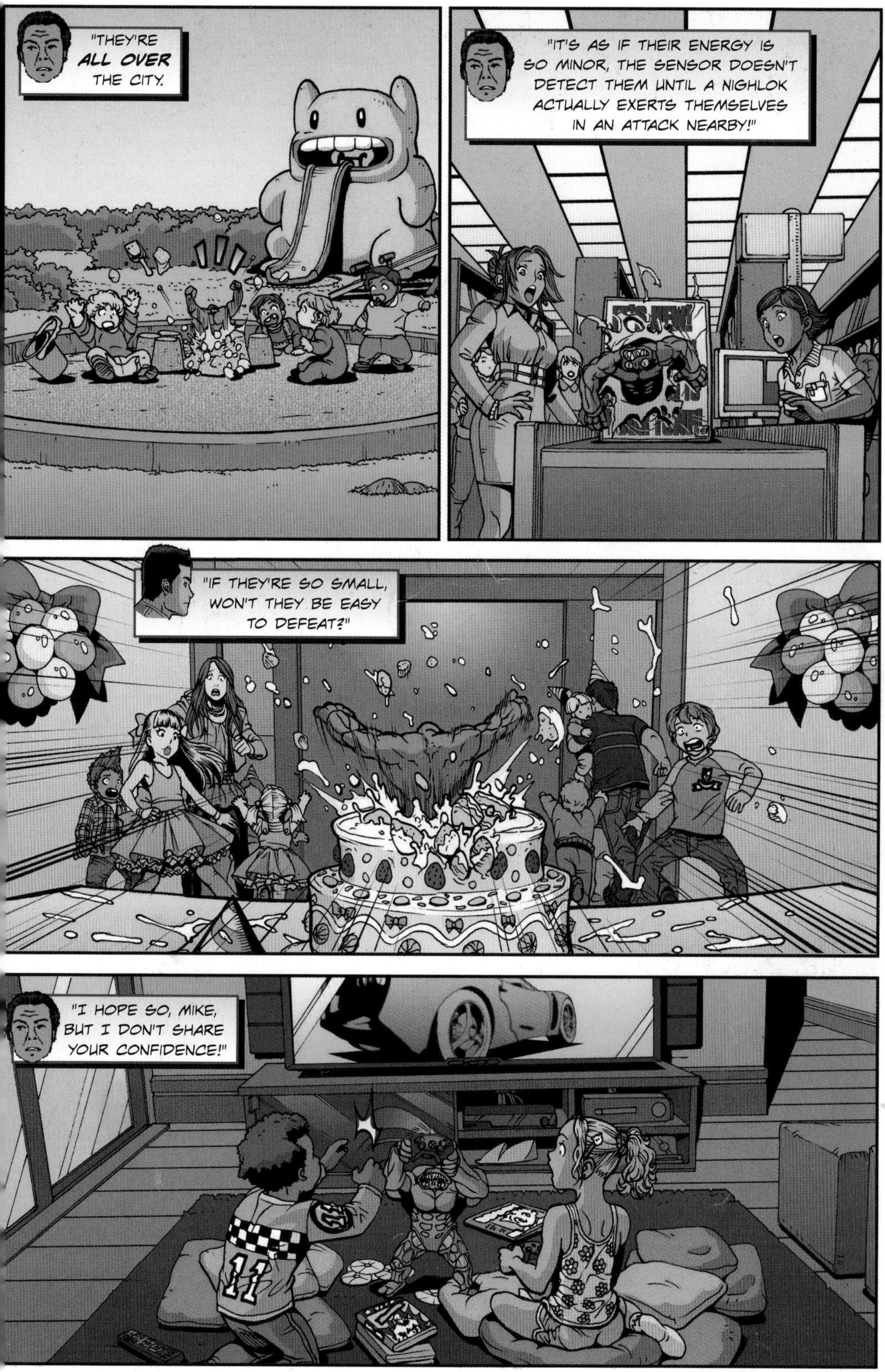
"THEY'RE ALL OVER THE CITY.
"IT'S AS IF THEIR ENERGY IS SO MINOR, THE SENSOR DOESN'T DETECT THEM UNTIL A NIGHLOK ACTUALLY EXERTS THEMSELVES IN AN ATTACK NEARBY!"
"IF THEY'RE SO SMALL, WON'T THEY BE EASY TO DEFEAT?"
"I HOPE SO, MIKE, BUT I DON'T SHARE YOUR CONFIDENCE!"

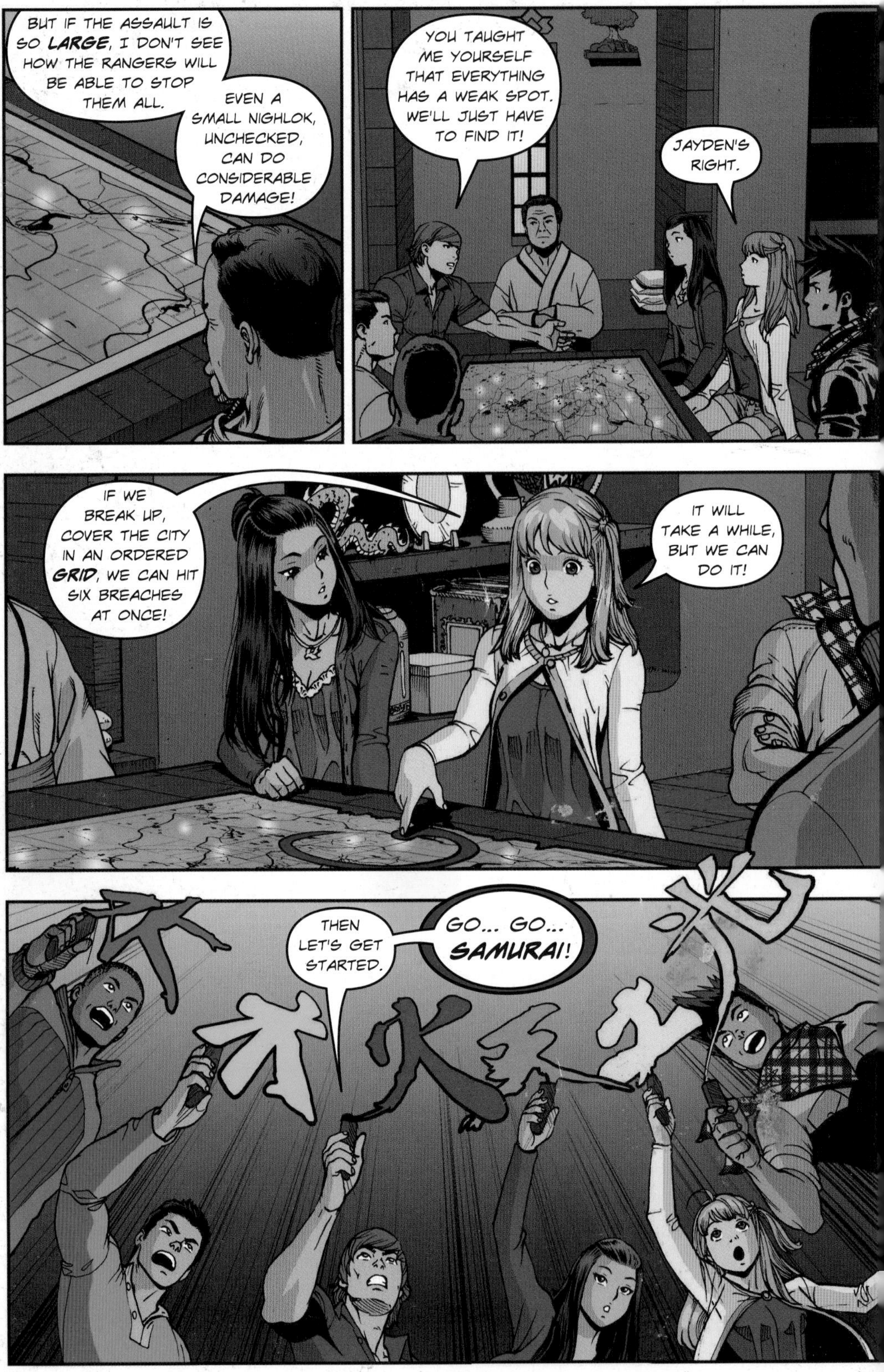
BUT IF THE ASSAULT IS SO **LARGE**, I DON'T SEE HOW THE RANGERS WILL BE ABLE TO STOP THEM ALL.
EVEN A SMALL NIGHLOK, UNCHECKED, CAN DO CONSIDERABLE DAMAGE!
YOU TAUGHT ME YOURSELF THAT EVERYTHING HAS A WEAK SPOT. WE'LL JUST HAVE TO FIND IT!
JAYDEN'S RIGHT.
IF WE BREAK UP, COVER THE CITY IN AN ORDERED **GRID**, WE CAN HIT SIX BREACHES AT ONCE!
IT WILL TAKE A WHILE, BUT WE CAN DO IT!
THEN LET'S GET STARTED.
GO... GO... **SAMURAI**!

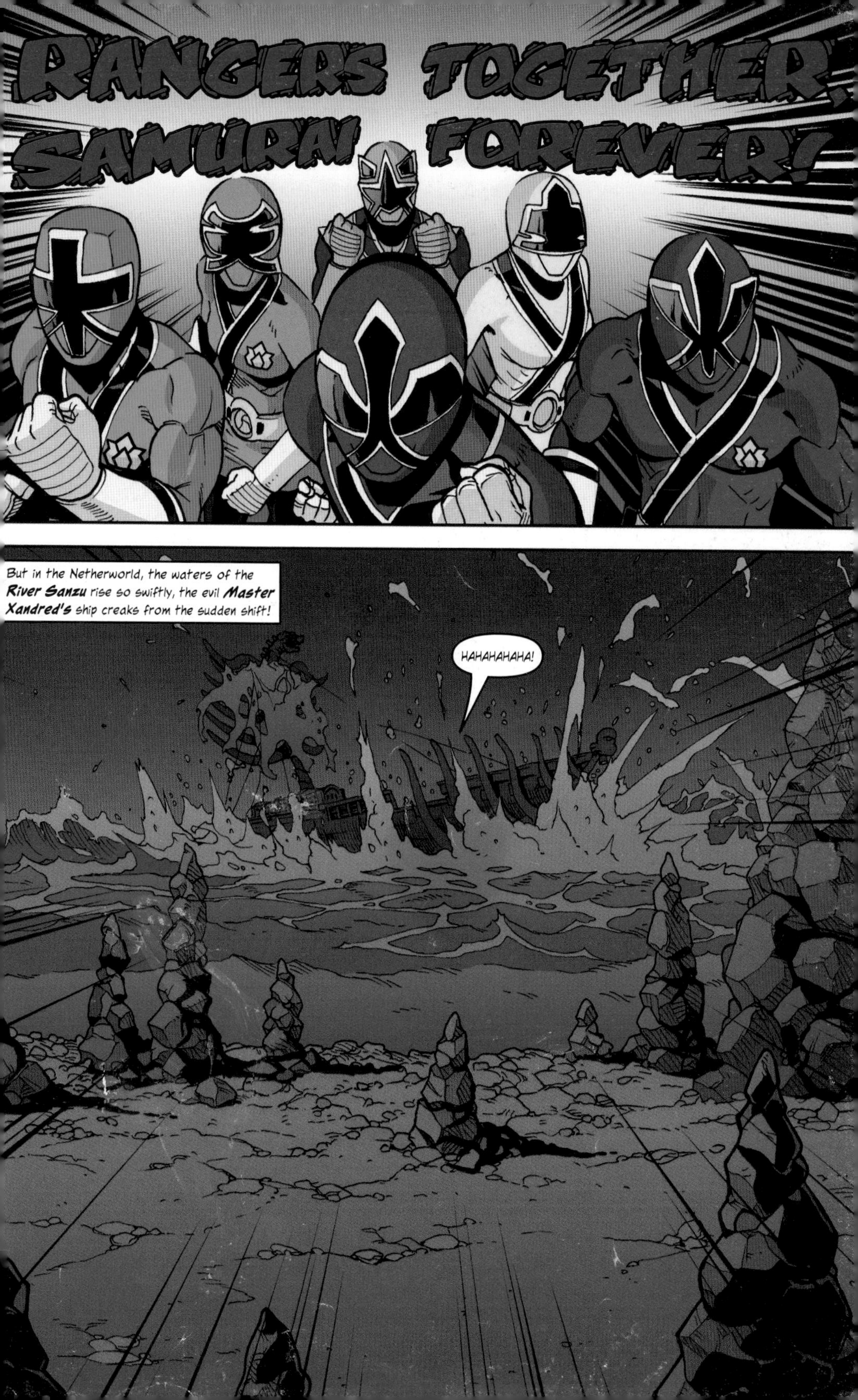
RANGERS TOGETHER, SAMURAI FOREVER!
But in the Netherworld, the waters of the River Sanzu rise so swiftly, the evil Master Xandred's ship creaks from the sudden shift!
HAHAHAHAHA!

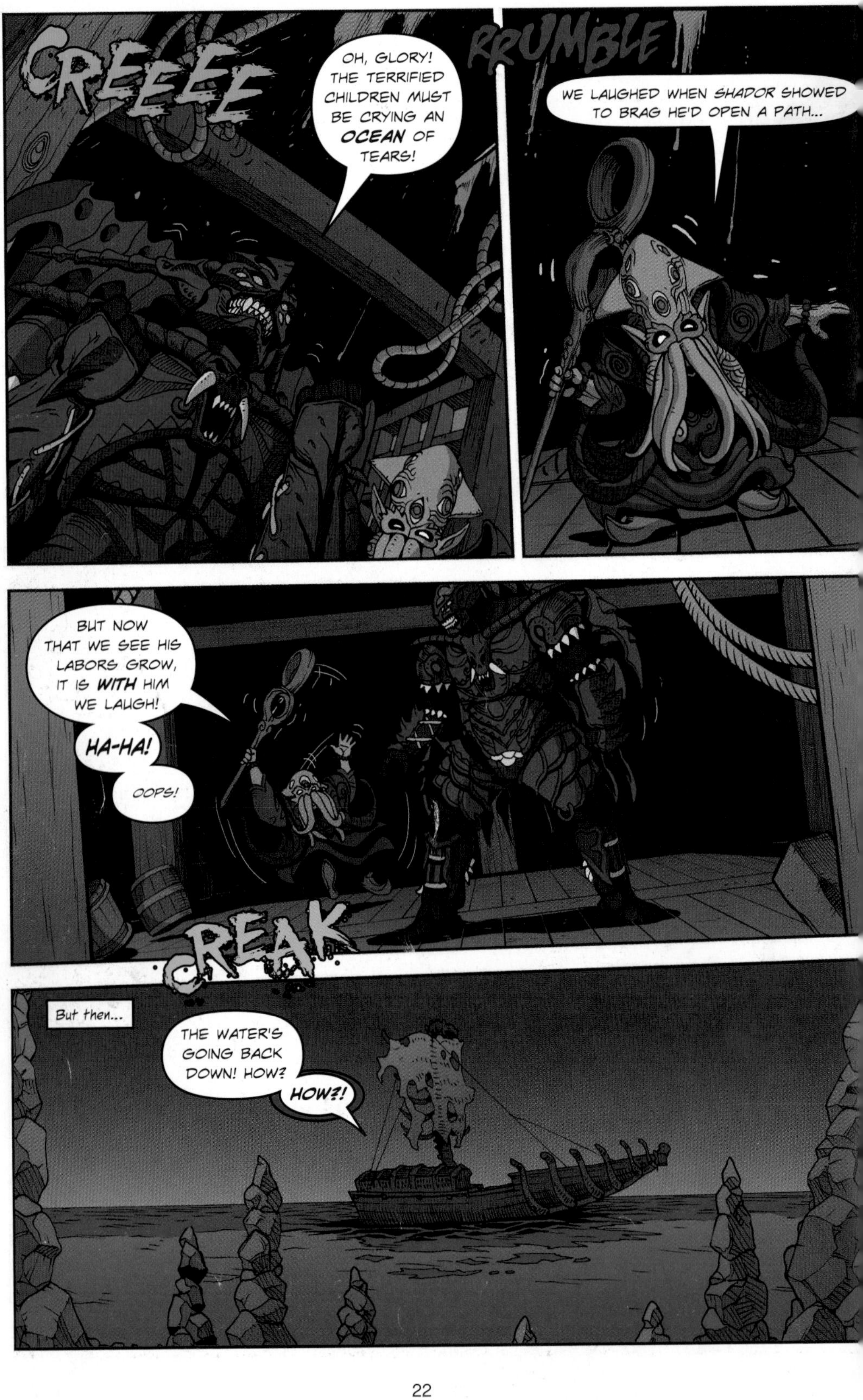
CREEEE
OH, GLORY! THE TERRIFIED CHILDREN MUST BE CRYING AN OCEAN OF TEARS!
RRUMBLE
WE LAUGHED WHEN SHADOR SHOWED TO BRAG HE'D OPEN A PATH...
BUT NOW THAT WE SEE HIS LABORS GROW, IT IS WITH HIM WE LAUGH!
HA-HA!
OOPS!
CREAK
But then...
THE WATER'S GOING BACK DOWN! HOW?
HOW?!

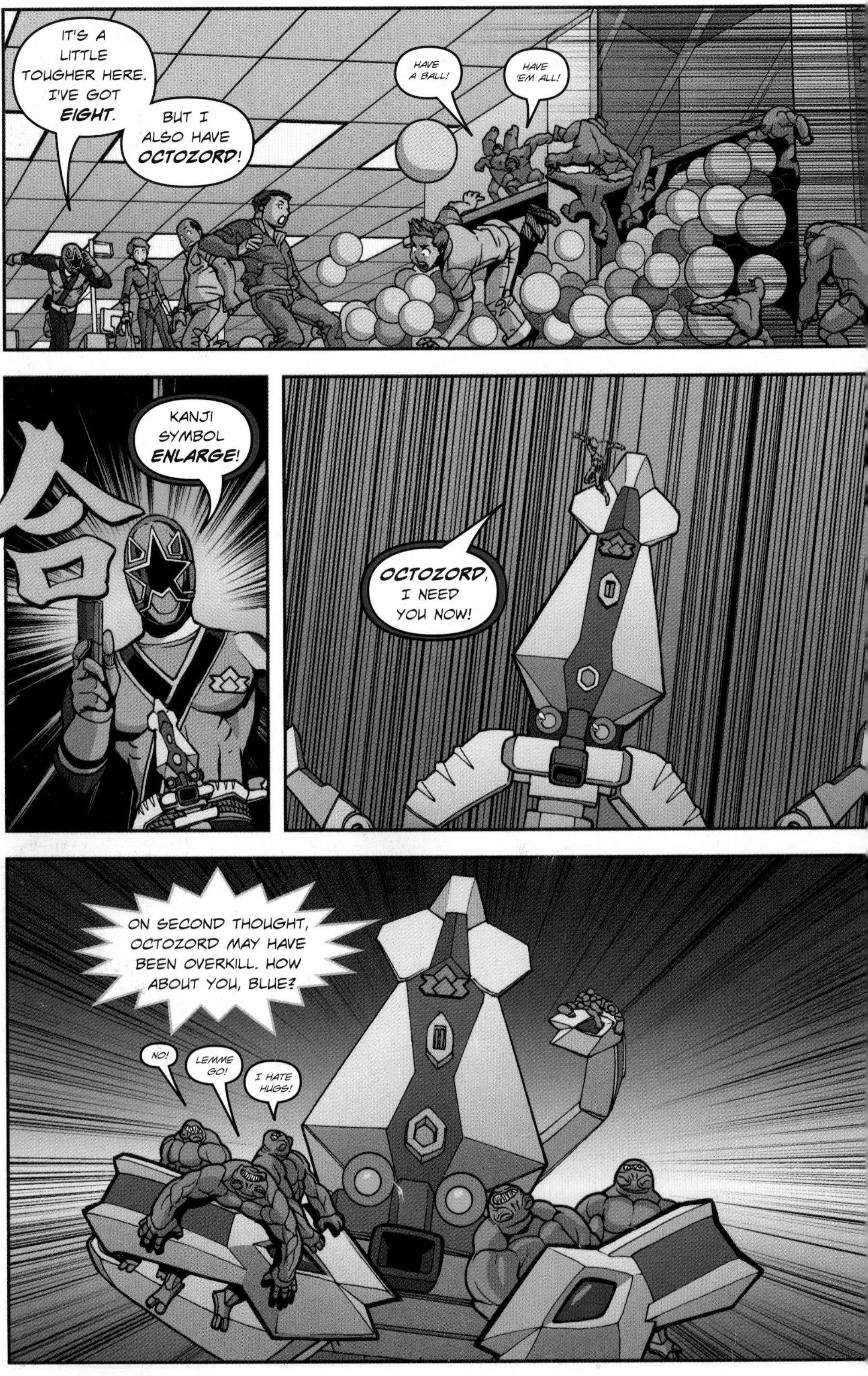
IT'S A LITTLE TOUGHER HERE. I'VE GOT EIGHT.
BUT I ALSO HAVE OCTOZORD!
HAVE A BALL!
HAVE 'EM ALL!
KANJI SYMBOL ENLARGE!
OCTOZORD, I NEED YOU NOW!
ON SECOND THOUGHT, OCTOZORD MAY HAVE BEEN OVERKILL. HOW ABOUT YOU, BLUE?
NO!
LEMME GO!
I HATE HUGS!

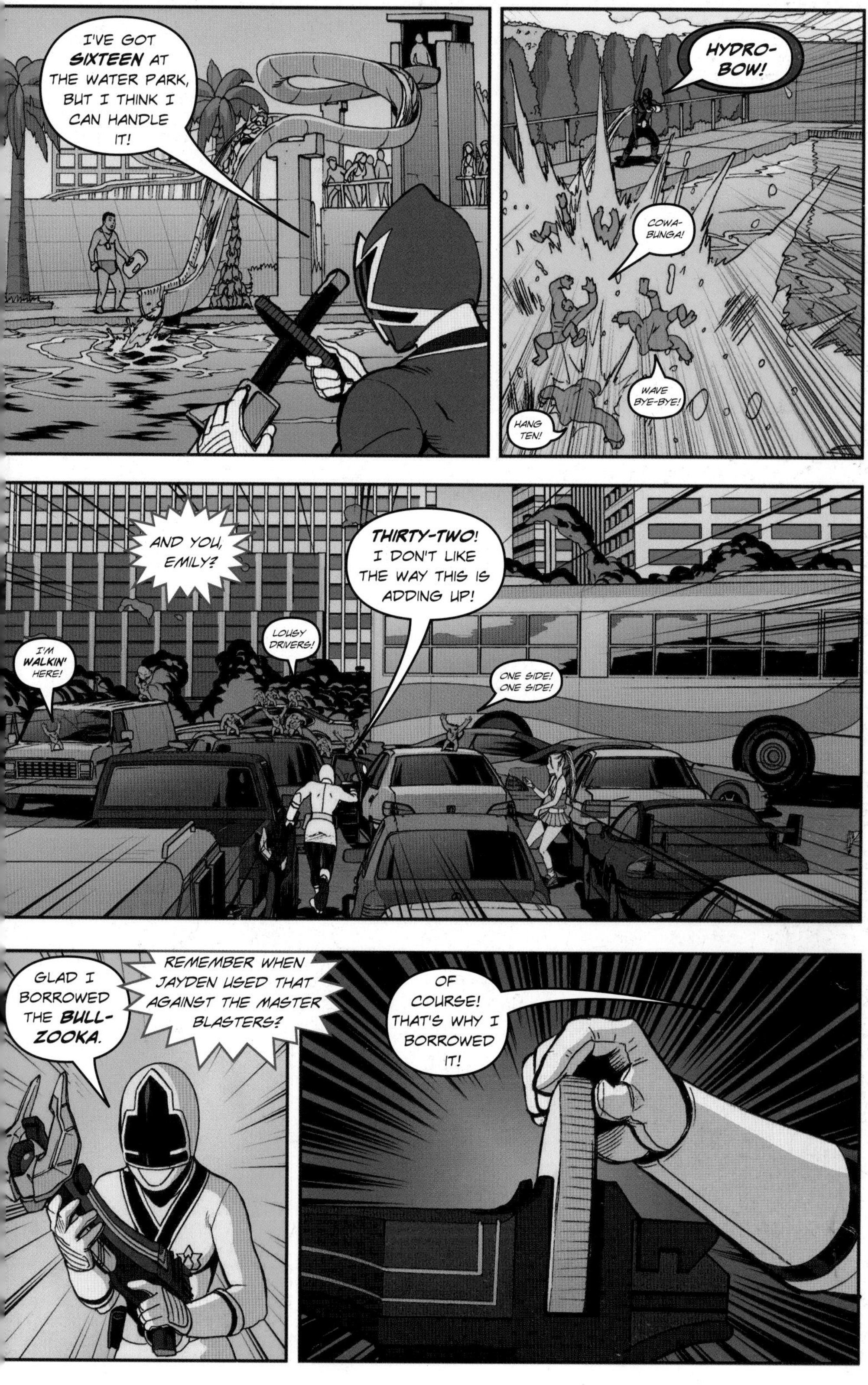
I'VE GOT SIXTEEN AT THE WATER PARK, BUT I THINK I CAN HANDLE IT!
HYDRO-BOW!
COWA-BUNGA!
WAVE BYE-BYE!
HANG TEN!
AND YOU, EMILY?
THIRTY-TWO! I DON'T LIKE THE WAY THIS IS ADDING UP!
I'M WALKIN' HERE!
LOUSY DRIVERS!
ONE SIDE! ONE SIDE!
GLAD I BORROWED THE BULL-ZOOKA.
REMEMBER WHEN JAYDEN USED THAT AGAINST THE MASTER BLASTERS?
OF COURSE! THAT'S WHY I BORROWED IT!

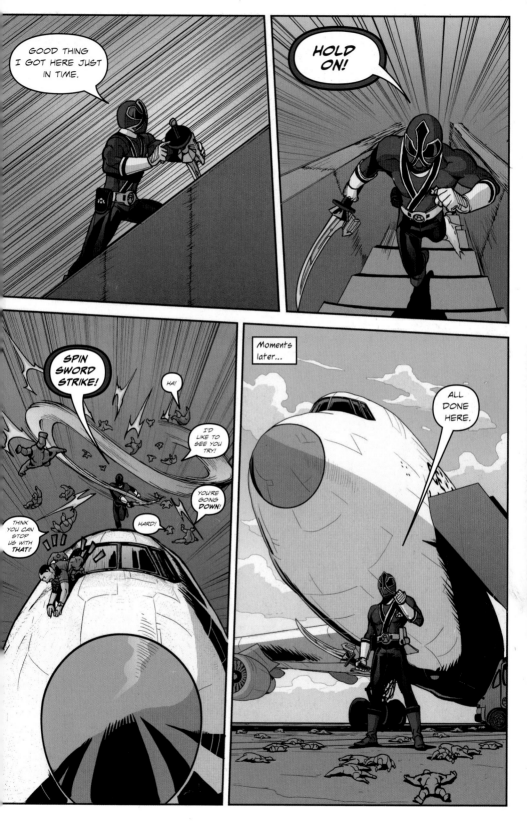

28

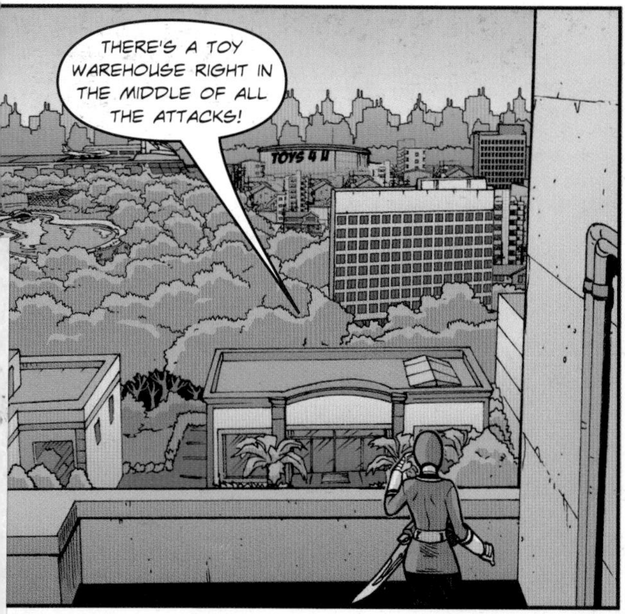
THERE'S A TOY WAREHOUSE RIGHT IN THE MIDDLE OF ALL THE ATTACKS!
TOYS 4 U

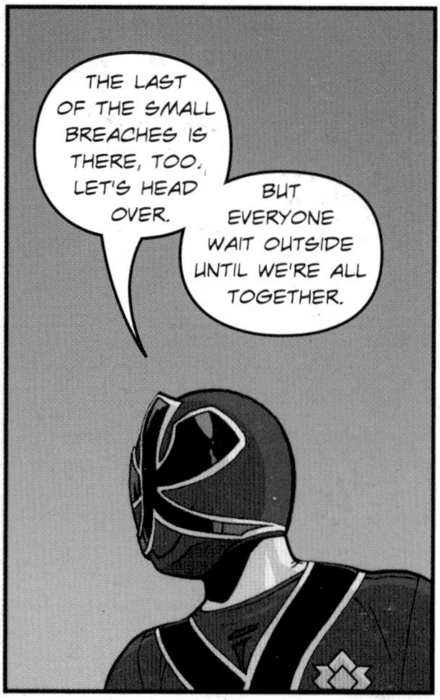
THE LAST OF THE SMALL BREACHES IS THERE, TOO. LET'S HEAD OVER.
BUT EVERYONE WAIT OUTSIDE UNTIL WE'RE ALL TOGETHER.

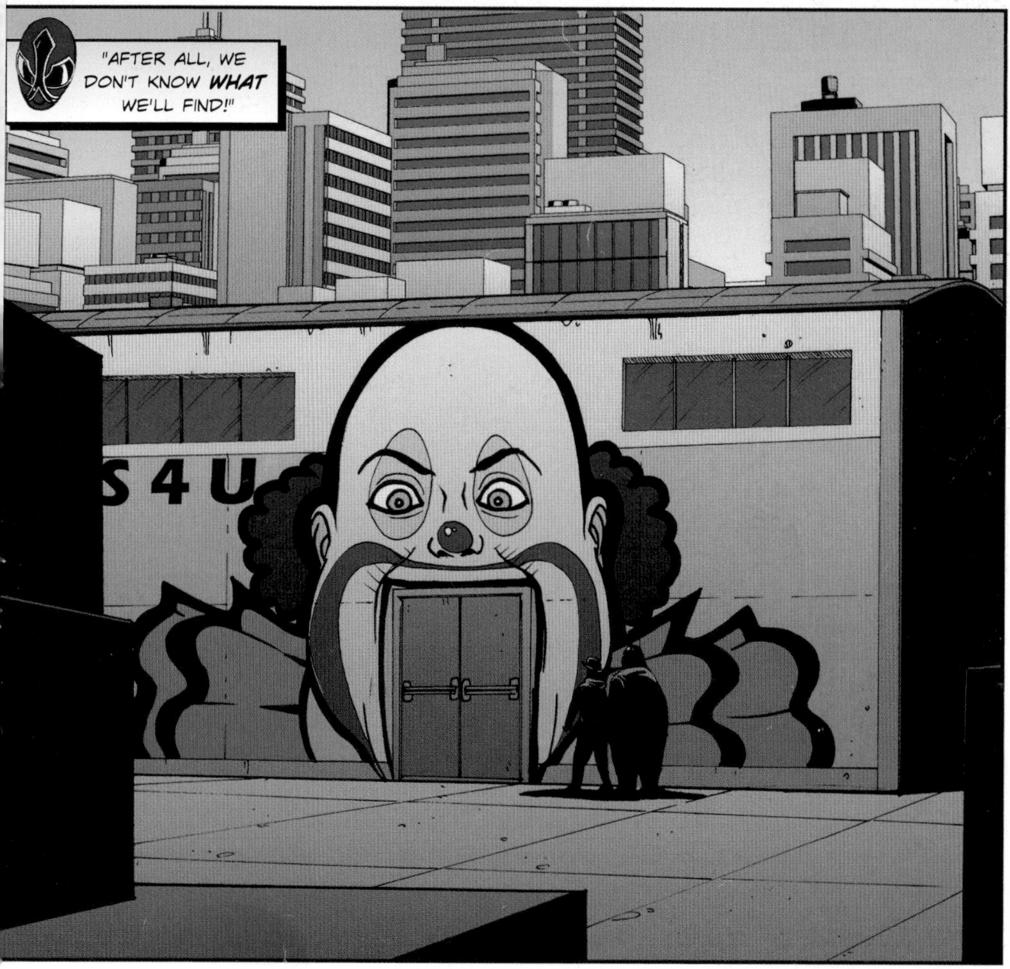
"AFTER ALL, WE DON'T KNOW **WHAT** WE'LL FIND!"
S 4 U

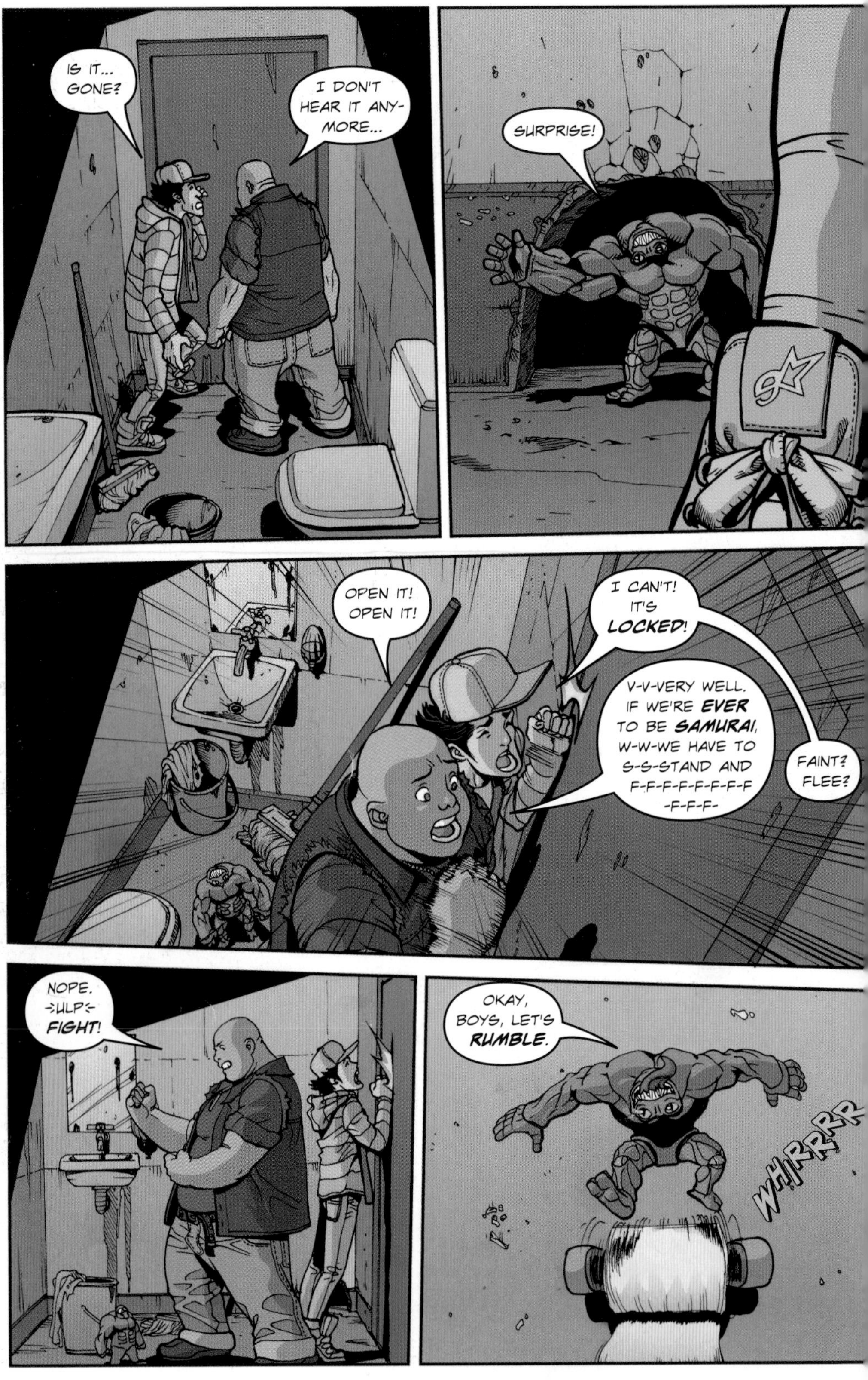
IS IT... GONE?
I DON'T HEAR IT ANY-MORE...
SURPRISE!
OPEN IT! OPEN IT!
I CAN'T! IT'S LOCKED!
V-V-VERY WELL. IF WE'RE EVER TO BE SAMURAI, W-W-WE HAVE TO S-S-STAND AND F-F-F-F-F-F-F-F -F-F-F-
FAINT? FLEE?
NOPE. ULP FIGHT!
OKAY, BOYS, LET'S RUMBLE.
WHIRRRR

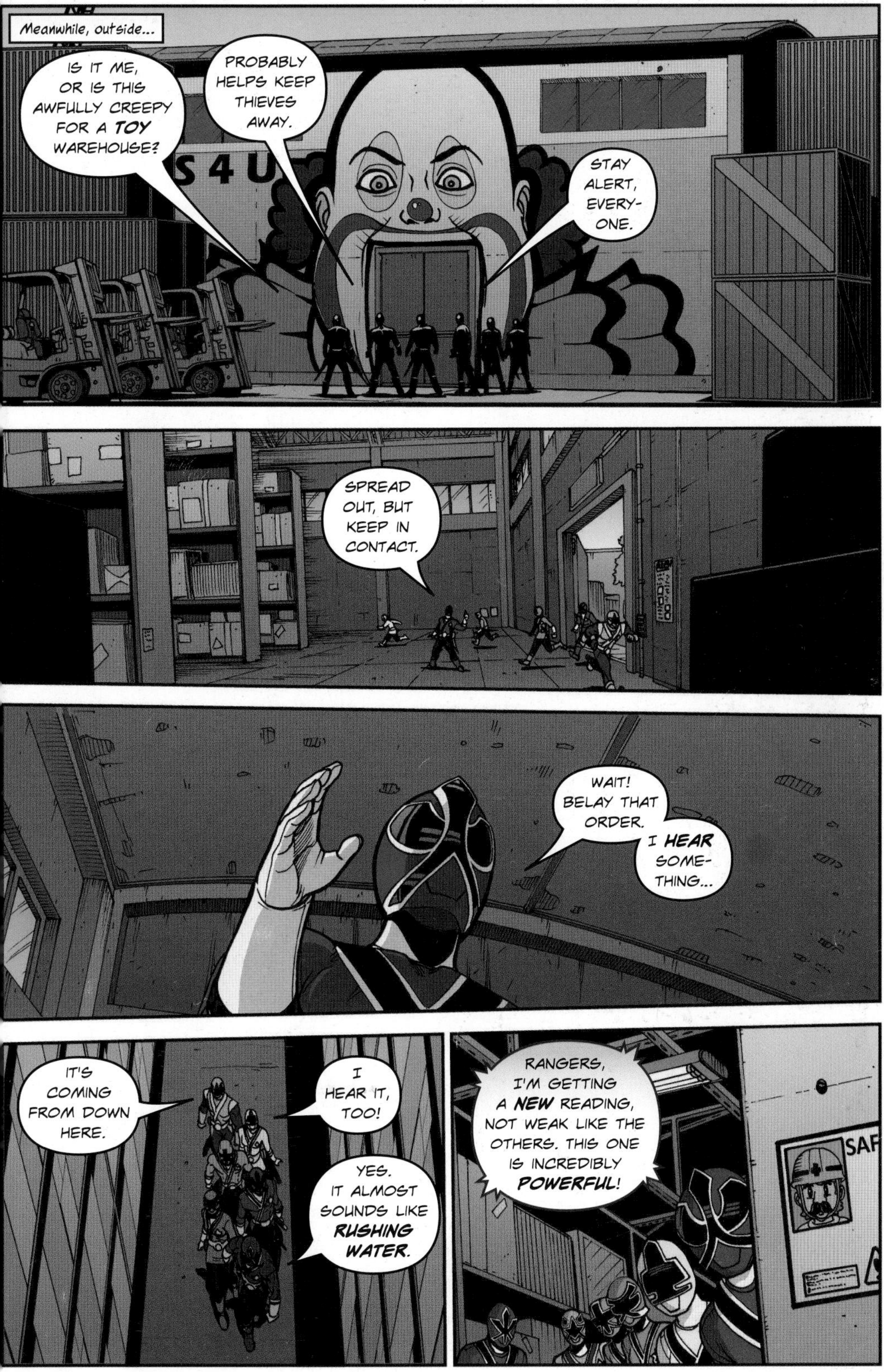
Meanwhile, outside...
IS IT ME, OR IS THIS AWFULLY CREEPY FOR A TOY WAREHOUSE?
PROBABLY HELPS KEEP THIEVES AWAY.
STAY ALERT, EVERY-ONE.
S 4 U
SPREAD OUT, BUT KEEP IN CONTACT.
WAIT! BELAY THAT ORDER.
I HEAR SOME-THING...
IT'S COMING FROM DOWN HERE.
I HEAR IT, TOO!
YES. IT ALMOST SOUNDS LIKE RUSHING WATER.
RANGERS, I'M GETTING A NEW READING, NOT WEAK LIKE THE OTHERS. THIS ONE IS INCREDIBLY POWERFUL!
SAF

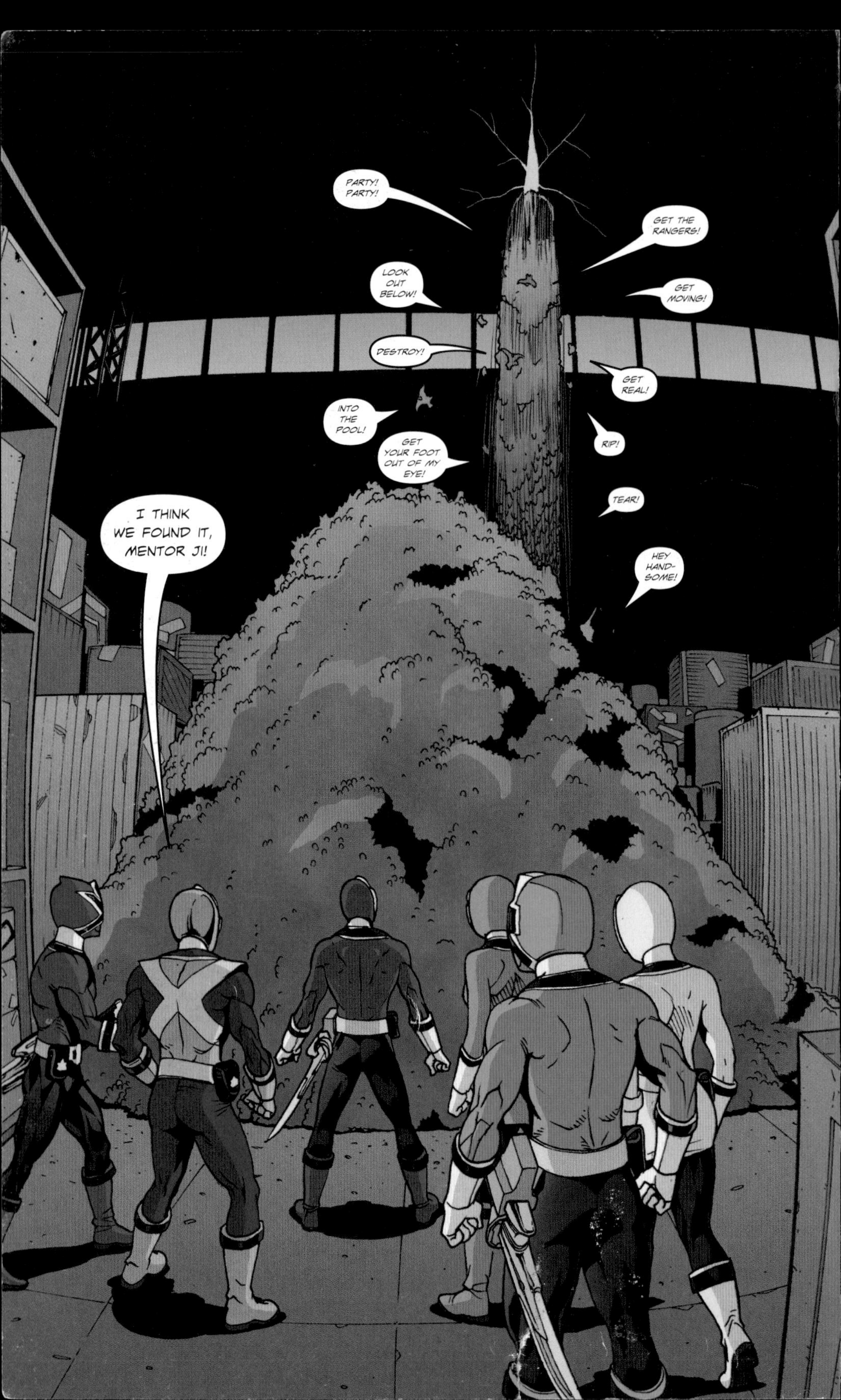
PARTY! PARTY!
GET THE RANGERS!
LOOK OUT BELOW!
GET MOVING!
DESTROY!
GET REAL!
INTO THE POOL!
GET YOUR FOOT OUT OF MY EYE!
RIP!
TEAR!
HEY HAND-SOME!
I THINK WE FOUND IT, MENTOR JI!

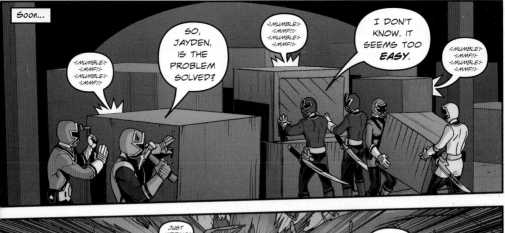

As the Rangers regroup, the thousands of small creatures race to a single spot on the warehouse floor!

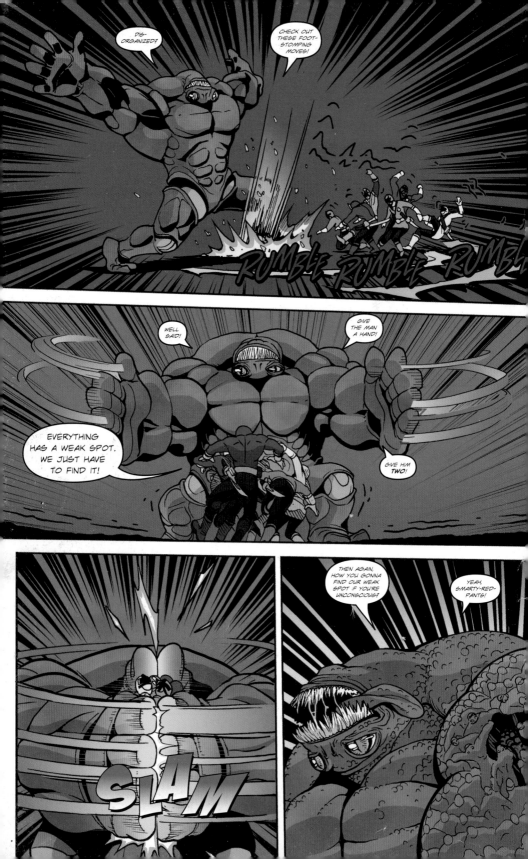

41

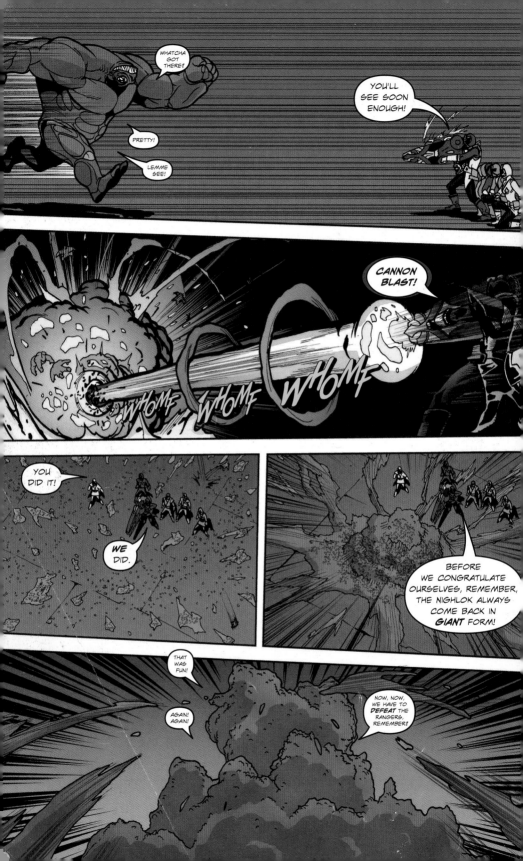

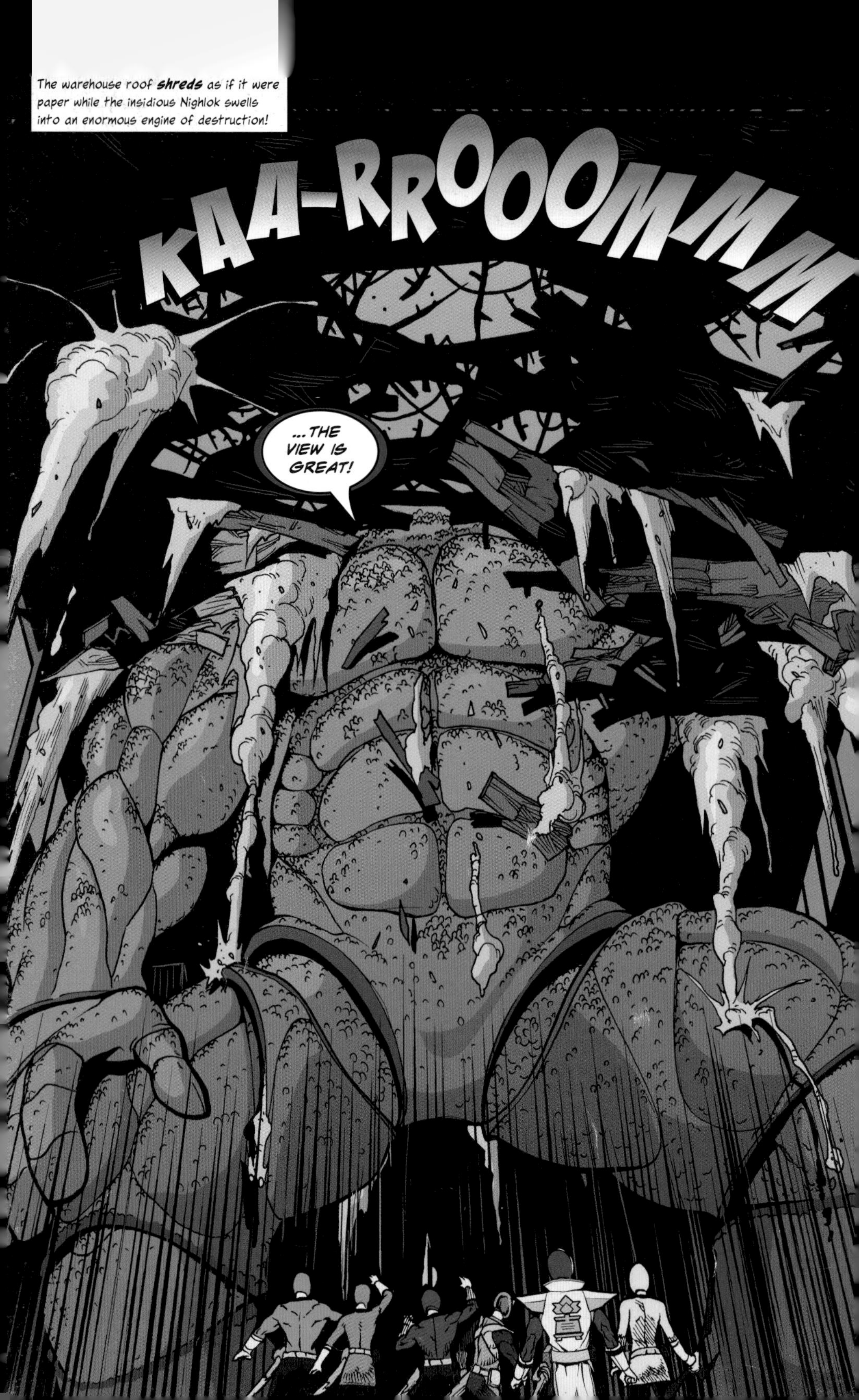
The warehouse roof shreds as if it were paper while the insidious Nighlok swells into an enormous engine of destruction!
KAA-RROOOOM-MM
...THE VIEW IS GREAT!

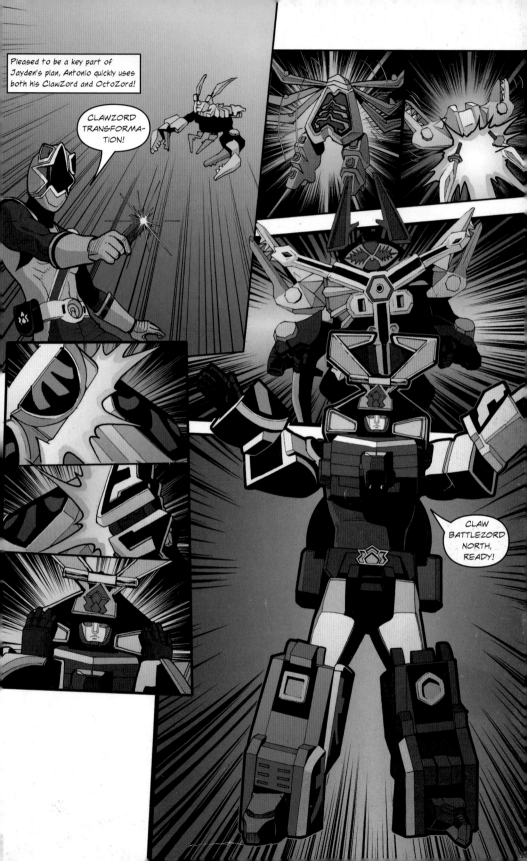

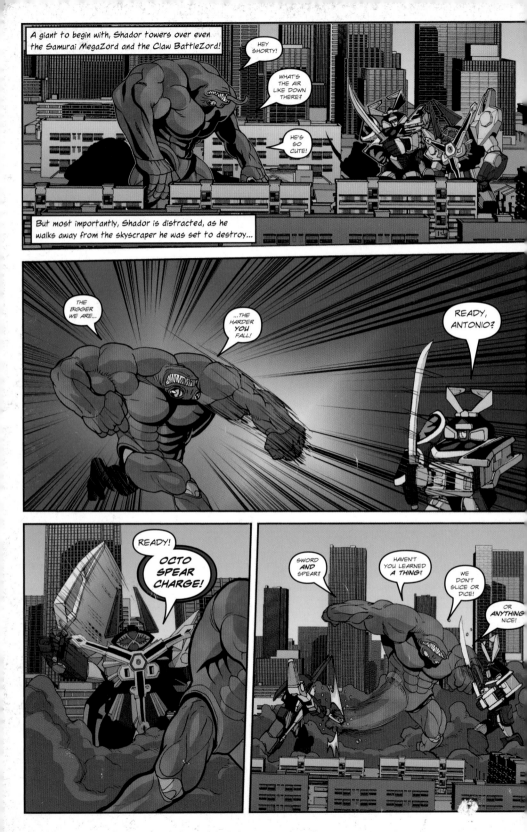

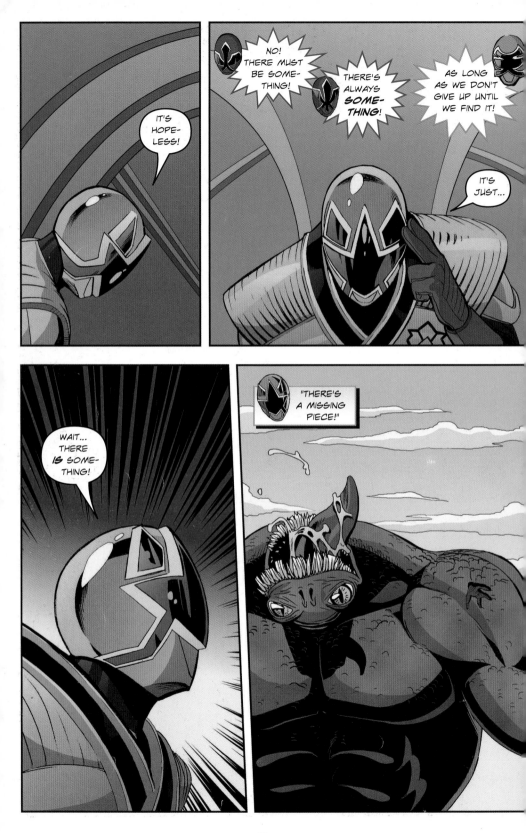

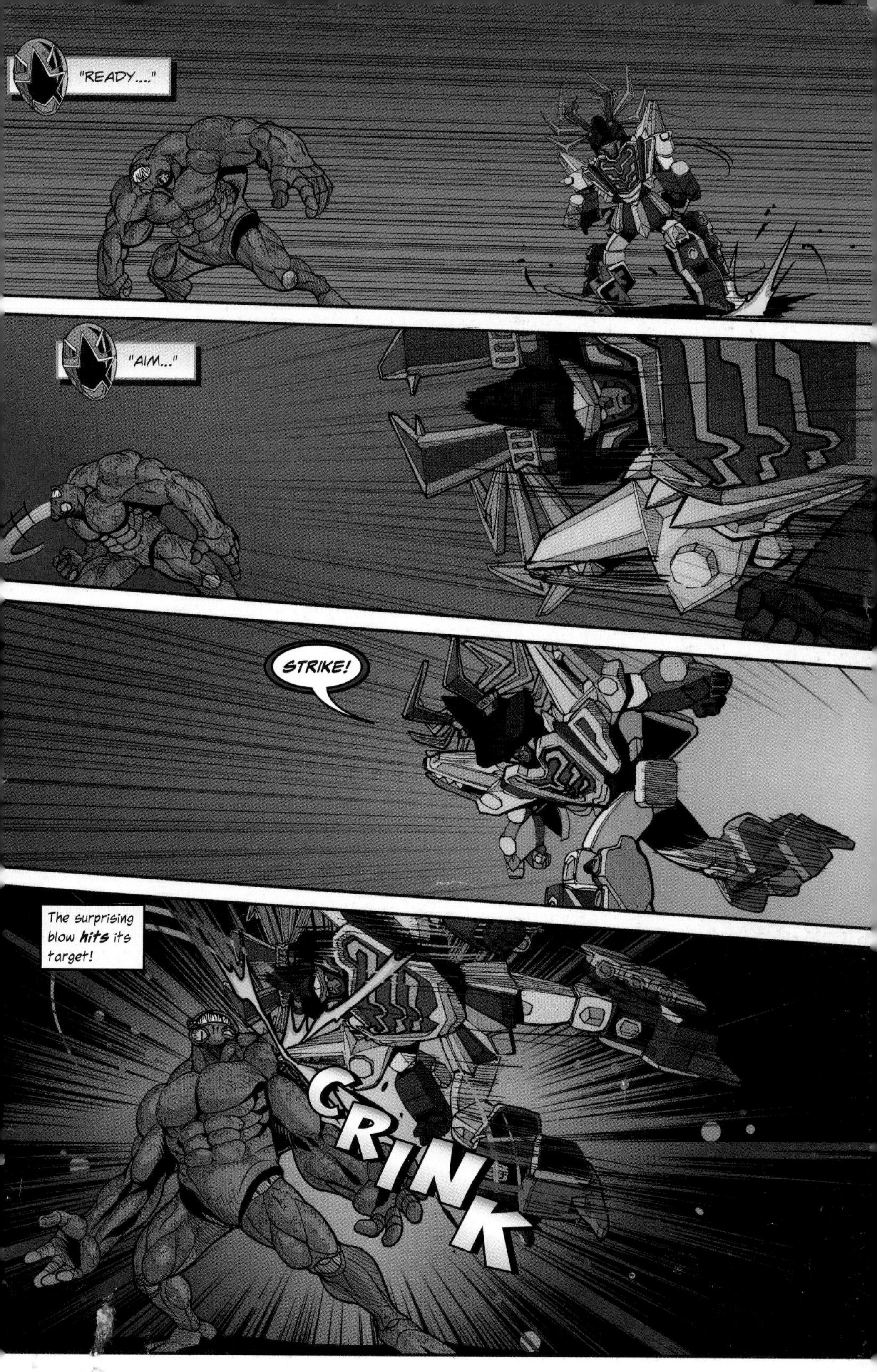
"READY...."
"AIM..."
STRIKE!
The surprising blow ***hits*** its target!
CRINK

WATCH OUT FOR PAPERCUTZ

Editor-in-Chief Jim Salicrup is ready to go into action with the
POWER RANGERS at the San Diego Comic-Con!

Welcome to the smashing second SABAN'S POWER RANGERS SUPER SAMURAI graphic novel series from Papercutz. I'm Jim Salicrup, the bleary-eyed EditorZord-in-Chief of Papercutz, the folks dedicated to creating great graphic novels for all ages. As promised last time, in our premiere POWER RANGERS SUPER SAMURAI graphic novel, here's a short bio of super-star artist Paulo Henrique...

Paulo Henrique

Paulo truly is an amazingly talented artist, and we're all thrilled to be working with him at Papercutz! Born in Sao Paolo, Brazil in 1979, he started his professional career drawing MEGAMAN comics for Brazilian publisher Magnum. Later, Paulo drew MYTH WARRIORS for Top Cow Productions, and illustrated volumes 6-20 of THE HARDY BOYS and volumes 1 and 2 of THE HARDY BOYS: THE NEW CASE FILES for Papercutz. Paulo drew volumes 1 and 2 of LEGO® NINJAGO both of which were runaway hits. When approached to draw the POWER RANGERS series, he said it was a "dream job" for him. He lives in Brazil where he is also a musician, and loves watching THE SIMPSONS.

Associate Editor Michael Petranek (third from the right) with the
cast of SABAN'S POWER RANGERS SUPER SAMURAI

Recently, Papercutz Associate Editor Michael Petranek attended POWER
MORPHICON, a convention just for POWER RANGERS fans, and filed this mini-report

Michael with Jason A. Narvy
and Paul Schrier

I had a great time in Pasadena, California
attending the third annual Power Morphicon!
I brought 1,000 exclusive to-the-show POWER
RANGERS mini comics and a few hundred posters,
and they were all gone by the first day! I met several
past and current cast members including Jason A.
Narvy and Paul Schrier (Skull and Bulk), along with
the cast of POWER RANGERS SUPER SAMURAI.
It was a lot of fun to show the actors how Paulo
depicts them in the comics, and I found then all to
be very warm and friendly. It was very hard keeping
a straight face next to Paul – he had me laughing
nonstop! The actors enjoyed seeing themselves in
comics, and I enjoyed my time with all of them. It
was a great show!

I want to thank Umesh Patel at Ranger Crew for introducing me to so many
fans, and Saban, without which none of this would have been possible! Thanks to
everyone who attended.

As you can tell we're all excited about the POWER RANGERS, and like you, we can't
wait till our next POWER RANGERS graphic novel coming soon! Be sure not to miss it

Thanks,

JiM

STAY IN TOUCH!

EMAIL: papercutz@papercutz.com
WEB: www.papercutz.com
TWITTER: @papercutzgn
FACEBOOK: PAPERCUTZGRAPHICNOVELS
REGULAR MAIL: Papercutz, 160 Broadway, Suite 700, East Wing,
                    New York, NY 10038